For April, a saint for putting up with me. Thank you for everything you do to help me see my dreams.

In Memory of David Farland.
Beloved and irreplaceable mentor of so many.

COERCED

BOOK THREE OF THE ANGELSONG SERIES

KEVIN A DAVIS

COERCED

CONTENTS

This is *Coerced,* Book Three of the AngelSong series. The story of Haddie, her dad, and her friends who have stumbled into the plots of the Unceasing.

A law student in Eugene, Oregon, Haddie and her father have the power to spread matter back into time. They might be unique, but not alone.

They have survived so far, but how long can their luck hold out?

PART 1

We have to take action if we want to live in this misguided world.

As HADDIE SAT in her cubicle in the back, the chime to the front door of the office rang; she tilted her head absently to find a yellow haze visible through the wall. *A coerced*, she thought. Jumping to her feet, she nearly upset her morning tea.

The back office of the law firm had an open space between Haddie's cubicle and the wall that bordered the reception area. Heart-pounding, she stared over the pile of banker boxes which had grown since Josh had been on his extended hiatus.

Having one of the coerced walk in the front door betrayed any sense of sanctuary her job had ever presented. The glowing yellow haze was only visible to her. Sitting in the cubicle behind her, Grace, the firm's paralegal, would likely think Haddie's reaction strange.

This can't be happening. Haddie sucked in a breath. She smelled coffee over the musty scents of paper and cardboard.

The coerced moved deeper into the lobby, the yellow haze tracking along the wall. Surely they had come for her.

I'm trapped. The law firm had one door in the front, and the kitchen door that she'd never make without being seen. Beyond Grace's cubicle, the copy room offered a place to hide, but Toby was already exposed at her reception desk. Haddie couldn't just leave her to the coerced.

The yellow haze continued across the reception area, rising and falling with its steps. Haddie couldn't move; she just stood in her cubicle and watched the wall.

"Hi, Josh. You're back." Toby's voice, happy and tinged with surprise, echoed through the hall in front of Haddie.

Josh? Did the coerced come in with him? Toby didn't sound alarmed. The yellow haze approached the reception desk. From her cubicle, Haddie could see down the hall to the edge of the lobby opening where Toby sat. *I've got to do something.*

"Hi, Toby. Good to be back." Josh's voice sounded odd. Too normal. The usual playfulness gone; he sounded ordinary.

Haddie waited, expecting some introduction of a second person in the lobby, but the yellow haze moved toward the entrance to the hall. *It is Josh.* Someone had coerced him. Blood rushed up her face, warming her cheeks, and anger replaced some of the panic. This couldn't be coincidence; it had to be because of her. Had they sent him to kill her? Could she defend herself against someone she knew? She'd never considered what she would do if one of her friends were coerced. *This is my fault.*

She tracked him as he walked down the hall, turned the corner, and headed toward her.

"Haddie?" Grace sat in her cubicle with her hands over the keyboard. Her dark, delicate features didn't frown, but concern showed in her eyes.

"Josh —" Haddie started. What could she say? He's

been coerced, brain-washed? Controlled by someone with powers? It would sound insane.

Grace shrugged. "He's back. We had a couple weeks of peace. I wonder what his story will be?" She misunderstood Haddie's reaction.

The yellow glow paused, still hidden in the hallway. Andrea, their boss, spoke, with a jovial but muffled tone. Josh moved into her office and their voices were dampened by the wall.

Haddie composed her face and sat. She held the edge of her desk and kept her eyes on the haze. *He's not here to kill me.* Josh wouldn't have visited their boss first if he intended to attack. What then — to spy on her? At least she wouldn't have to defend herself, yet. Who did this to him? Who would have sent him? Did they know about her involvement with Dad in Boise? *I have to tell Dad.* The others would need to know.

Absently, Haddie touched her phone.

Grace chuckled from the other side of their cubicle wall. "Who would come back to work on a Friday? Might as well take the weekend."

Josh stepped out of Andrea's office and took the last few paces of the hall to their back office. "Hi, Haddie. Hi, Grace."

Tiny sparks of yellow light buzzed around and through his face, like a swarm of insects. They made his blond hair look dull and dark in comparison. He moved past with a smile and headed for his cubicle. He wore a T-shirt and jeans with sneakers. Everything about him screamed wrong.

"That's it? Hi?" Grace sounded incredulous. She continued when he didn't respond. "Okay. There's three boxes from the DA that need to get scanned. Haddie stacked them along your cubicle."

"Thanks. I'll get to them in a minute." Josh dropped down behind cubicle walls, and the glow shone through.

Haddie could hear his chair squeak, and it sounded like he powered up his computer. Usually, he would have gone directly to the copy room and begun scanning. How much of Josh did the coercion leave? She shuddered and touched her phone again. Dad had to know about this.

Without thinking, she turned on her cell and saw the text she'd sent to David. "I overreacted. Do you want to talk?" She'd forced David into giving her space, and he'd respected her request. *Had he moved on?* She wanted to be with him, but was it fair to him? All the secrets? What if she were immortal like Dad? How did her dad handle it? She had sent the text anyway, perhaps selfishly. David hadn't responded. *Maybe he did move on.*

She wouldn't text Dad on her cell anyway; the police and FBI were still looking for him. Haddie leaned down and got the burner phone from her purse. She tilted back in her chair and watched her cubicle walls and Josh's face glowing through them. "Josh, one of my coworkers, is coerced. I'm freaking out. What do I do?" She sent the text to her dad and waited a second; if he wasn't riding, he tended to respond immediately.

Come on Dad. The documents that she'd been reviewing waited on her computer screen. Andrea hadn't put her on anything too important, and now that Josh would be doing scanning, she could take off without any repercussions. The others needed to know about this. Whoever controlled Josh had gotten close to Haddie for a reason. However, he had barely looked at her, let alone talk to her. Josh seemed more interested in his computer than anything else. What was he looking at?

Haddie could get up, make up a pretext to go over to his cubicle, and look at his screen. She shivered at the thought.

I can't get near him. She wouldn't be able to control her expression.

Josh didn't pose an immediate danger, but she had to do something. Dad had been her first thought. She could check with Sam. She and Meg wouldn't be out riding, they'd be working the dogs — training or exercising them at the farm — whatever it is they did under Dad's new business. Sam would know if Dad had taken off for a ride.

I need to let Kiana know about this. Maybe Haddie could slip out and meet with everyone.

CHAPTER 2

THOMAS RODE his black '47 Knucklehead south toward Eugene with a dull roar. He preferred the mountain highways that everyone avoided. A hot midsummer's day made for a perfect ride. The wind kept him cool on the long stretches, and he'd wound through some beautiful hills before he'd entered the Willamette Valley. His route to Creswell took him through flat farmlands where the air smelled like hot grass. Small mountains broke over the trees on the horizon. His trip had been pleasant.

As he skirted the east side of Eugene, he ran into some of the hurried drivers racing against their clocks. He didn't miss Goshen, but he still grieved losing Haddie. She wasn't ready to leave her friends and start a new life. Detective Cooper still harassed her. Grinding away at city living, she seemed to enjoy and thrive on the hectic pace and constant interruptions. He could remember times, centuries ago, when he'd found small pleasures in city life. *Not anymore.*

Sam and Meg had taken well to the country, as long as he had customers with dogs to board, train, and enjoy. The rural area west of Bend looked much like the farms he passed, except it had more trees. Around Creswell, most of the forests were young. The trees had been replanted or grew back after the lumber companies had come through. Thomas had already begun his own replanting of oak, red alder, and red cedar on the farmlands he'd bought. Sam had grown fond of dogwood and swore it had to do with the flowers, not the name.

Creswell began with houses tucked on the edges of farms with fences, gardens, and driveways with trucks. In a short minute, the farms dwindled and the homes took over. Businesses tucked between or sprouted off the sides of family residences. He rumbled across the overpass at I-5, trading the warm natural scents for fumes. He was thankful that his Knucklehead overpowered the sounds of the city.

Few clouds dotted the bright blue sky over the traffic light as Thomas pulled through, slowing at the corner of the entrance to the RV park. The takeout restaurant had a car under an old gas station overhang. He rumbled into the RV park and veered north for the wooden shack of an office. Miguel's beat-up brown Ford was parked out front.

Thomas pulled beside the truck and killed the bike. He stretched his aching joints as he got off, checking the surroundings for any unusual cars or people. He'd used this drop-off for years, mainly because of the exits it offered a motorcycle where a car couldn't follow.

He opened the office door with the creaking hinge, and the smell of chorizo and coffee welcomed him. The soda cooler whined in the corner.

"Hey, Mr. Regis, back so soon? Nice day for a ride." Miguel nodded toward the window.

"I'll be back and forth a bit, got work in Reno," Thomas lied, wiping his hair back. He'd gotten the USPS alert last night. It could only be Crocus. Angel had been lost during the fiasco in Boise last month. "Got anything for me?"

Miguel nodded. "You got something yesterday."

Thomas waited until Miguel found his box. He hadn't expected any messages. Last he'd heard from Crocus, the people tracking Meg had disappeared. They'd withdrawn right after Boise. It had been a relief and the only blessing that came from the debacle. Had something changed?

"Here it is." Miguel handed him an envelope. *The wrong envelope.*

Thomas paused for a second before taking it. His heart raced. "I appreciate it, Miguel. Take it easy today." He smiled and then moved to the window to open the too long envelope.

The parking lot remained empty. No FBI or police had moved along the street leading into the park. Crocus understood the protocols. Someone else had sent him a message. Who?

The folded sheet inside had "Lt. Tempest" written on it. Someone had gotten to Crocus or Angel. Likely Angel. They also seemed to know of his identity during the Vietnam War, though he'd been a lieutenant over a century before that as well.

Miguel's chair squeaked as he settled back down, and Thomas glanced again out the window before unfolding the letter. It was handwritten in a tight script without a signature, just a post office box in Texas.

"I hope this correspondence finds you well and you do not find my method of introduction too alarming. I had hoped to plead with you face to face, but your recent furlough has made that impossible. I've admired your work since I first heard of your skills while we both served in South Asia. Our work there served as a catalyst and an inspiration to bring me to the conclusions that drive my passion and mission today. I can only hope to persuade you to join me in this endeavor, a revolution against the afflictions of this present society."

Thomas stopped, checking outside. *They know about Vietnam.* The author was military, likely in the war as well. *I'd been foolish there. Too many witnesses.*

"When we first came to this world, many of us saw it as a paradise. We were young then, the nine of us. Our minds had been trained by our elders to further their purpose, their will. As youth, we sought our passions, our purposes, our will. Finding fault with our freedoms, the Gatekeepers, the Seroveilm, named us when they locked us here. Our nine, the Noveilm, lost our youngest, Makabetza, before we founded our kingdoms.

"The Seroveilm brought us here to protect the time-lines of this place from their enemy, and in abandoning us, forfeited this world. The Gates locked, so we have known only these wives and husbands, these children of ours. We must not squabble, as we have done in the past; it became our undoing. The blood of the Noveilm remains, brought out in our sacrifice and pain. I myself have used it wantonly, without purpose or mercy, and regret those harms but not what it has taught me. I have recalled my original purpose and will not sway from it again.

"We have to take action if we want to live in this misguided world."

Thomas continued reading to the end, then shook his head. Carefully folding the letter, he replaced it into the envelope and tucked it in an inside pocket of his jacket. *I'm exposed.* They could be waiting for him outside. The war had shifted. They focused on him, rather than his great-granddaughter Meg. Fair enough. Sweat moistened the insides of his gloves.

With an air of calm, he strode out to his bike. Smoothing back his hair, he put his helmet on. Still, he could see no parked car that seemed amiss. They could have rented a nearby building. Breathing in and out, he climbed on his bike and fired it up. Dust kicked up as he rolled it back and angled the front wheel.

Dropping into gear, he quickly rode through the park, not to the trailer he kept there, but down the road beside the office. He took a quick left and then veered right as the street curved.

No one seemed to follow.

The road led between trailers that ranged from gardened affairs to ratty boxes with children's toys scattered nearly to the street. It ended ahead, turning to rejoin the main street of the neighborhood. About three quarters down, Thomas turned sharply to the left and rode through the yard between two trailers, ignoring an indignant exclamation from an open window. A swale of grass led between a post office and a storage building. Rumbling between the two fenced areas, he pulled into the parking lot and headed for the street. Any car that tried to follow would have to exit the park elsewhere, and he would have a good lead on them. He scanned the sky for a drone or helicopter.

Turning north, he kept a close eye on the traffic behind. Nothing seemed suspicious, but he followed his exit plan and turned left. It would lead him through neighborhoods and country roads out and around Creswell, until he could be sure he wasn't being followed.

Was the mystery author's sole intent to reach out to him? The letter surely hadn't persuaded Thomas of anything, except that the writer had been unhinged. There would be no reply. *Concern, yes.*

This could be the same person who had killed his children and the families from his identity prior to Haddie's mother, the person who had caused Thomas to rescue Meg. They might also be behind the threat to Kiana, someone who could manipulate the FBI or a group within it to hunt one of their own agents. He'd even considered meeting Kiana, but that had become a personal interest. *I'll have to close it all down.* Anyone connected to Crocus or Angel would have to be suspect. He'd placed his investigators in a risk no one had suspected.

If the author found out about Haddie, she was an easy mark. He couldn't take any chances. He'd have to burn his phones and start over.

CHAPTER 3

Haddie returned from the kitchen with sensations against her palm from mixing the hot tea and ice. She entered the back room, veering widely so she could get a glimpse over the coerced Josh's shoulder.

He had an email open on his screen and didn't react to her approach. She couldn't read any details from her distance. *Is he catching up on missed emails?* That hardly seemed like Josh. No one bothered to email him because he rarely checked. *But it isn't really him, is it?*

Grace typed at her keyboard and didn't glance up as Haddie rerouted to her cubicle and sat with the tea. Cupping her hand on the cool bottom, she stared at her own work, hardly touched since Josh had come in. She'd tried while she waited. Dad hadn't responded, nor had Sam. There was some apprehension in that. She had almost alerted Kiana, but really wanted Dad's sound logic first. Why had he picked today to roam around the mountains on his bike? Sometimes she envied his relaxed life.

Her burner vibrated in her purse. Hopeful, Haddie put

down her glass, wiped wet hands across the sides of her work blouse, and leaned to retrieve it.

Liz. Haddie drew in a breath. Not Dad, but at least Liz wouldn't want to come up with a plan like Kiana might.

"Can you do this Sunday for an experiment? I've got a couple of ideas," Liz had texted.

The last thing Haddie wanted to do was use her power. She'd healed from Boise, but it had taken over two weeks. Now, with Josh showing up coerced, she couldn't focus on anything else.

She glanced at the yellow haze through the wall of her cubicle and began texting, "No. I've got a problem here. Josh came back to work, and he's been coerced. I can see it."

"No. The yellow glow thing?" Liz asked. Before Haddie could respond, Liz sent a second text. "You've got to get out of there. They've found you. When?"

"He didn't attack. He's going through emails on his computer." Haddie looked up at Josh's glow and twisted her hair.

"Whose email?"

Haddie raised her eyebrows. "His. I assumed."

"What if he's going through your work emails?"

Wouldn't he need her password? Haddie took a short breath, her chest felt tight. "How?"

"Ten different ways at least. Does he have any access? Does he work on the computers at all?"

Josh had been in the computer closet before. He sometimes helped the IT company Andrea had hired to do most of the work, and he had access to the network for scanning. He set permissions for Haddie to see files he scanned. Haddie tried to think what she might have sent via the company email that would matter. There had been a couple messages, back during the Harold Holmes case, but nothing too bad. She'd deleted those soon after. What was Josh looking for then?

"I don't think there's anything left on my company email that would matter." Haddie typed slowly.

"All right. If you're sure. How long has he been reading emails?" Liz asked.

"Two hours, but I don't know that he was reading emails all that time. He came in right after me and went straight to the computer. I've been freaking."

"Only use your computer for work. Get rid of your personal mail and don't browse anything. Terry might have other suggestions. I'm sick and my brain is mush."

Damn. Haddie closed her browser. Liz had been sick for the past two days, but she still went to work at the crime lab. Luckily, she wasn't teaching summer classes this year. Terry *would* be best at tech advice, especially considering that was his major. Besides, he loved conspiracies. He'd be ecstatic about this.

I can't leave Josh like this. Was there a way to fix him?

"What do you think about getting rid of the compulsion? Could that be possible?"

"You were able to resist powers with Sameedha, could that work?"

Haddie's face grew cold as she looked up. *Do I dare?* What if he noticed and went beserk? Not here. Her chest felt empty. *I don't want to be alone with him either.* Maybe Dad or Kiana could help.

Aaron. He had the coercion power, but didn't use it. Once, in his youth, he'd used it. They didn't talk about it. *He won't help.* He'd run when Kiana had been shot. Haddie had kept Aaron's secret, even from Liz. Dad, she had told.

Liz's advice seemed the best so far. Haddie could barely

think. "I could try, but I'd want Dad or Kiana with me," Haddie texted.

She twisted her hair into a knot around her right hand. The thought of triggering Josh into someone she might have to defend herself from made her queasy. Dad might see it differently. Her regular cell vibrated. *David.* Haddie's hand got tangled in her hair as she jumped to open the message.

"Yes, I'd like to talk. Sometime Sunday? Tea?" David had responded.

Haddie nodded to herself and texted back, "Sunday tea would be great." She wanted to talk things out with David, and at least he hadn't completely given up on her, but Josh had her distracted. Maybe by Sunday she wouldn't be so freaked. Liz texted on the other phone, but Haddie hurried to text a second comment to David first. "We can text in the morning and pick a time." She winced, wanting to say thanks. *That would be odd.* She added a happy emoji instead.

Haddie moved back to her conversation with Liz on the other phone.

"What if it's not about you? What if Josh is looking for something on Harold Holmes? You said some group in the FBI was obsessed with finding him, the same people after Kiana. Sameedha and Barbara used coerced and were likely connected, what if this is all one big group and they want Harold Holmes?"

Why would they want Harold Holmes? The interest had always seemed a little odd. Even if they guessed what he could do, what would be the point in finding him? It didn't really matter since Harold Holmes and his brother Dmitry were both long gone. Dmitry had been the first person Haddie had killed.

Andrea stepped from the hall into the back room, and

Haddie jumped. She had two phones on her desk and barely any work done over the past couple of hours. Haddie looked up, forcing an innocent smile. One of the phones vibrated.

"Grace, a minute?" Andrea looked over to Josh's cubicle. "Let's get those boxes scanned in, Josh."

Josh replied, strangely professional. "Yes. Before lunch."

Grace stood, glancing over at Haddie, then followed Andrea. Haddie pushed her phone aside and grabbed her mouse. *I need to get some work done.* She had lunch coming up soon and planned on heading to the house on the hill where Kiana and Aaron were staying. Hopefully Dad would respond before then. *I should let Kiana know what's going on.*

CHAPTER 4

AARON LOOKED up from his laptop as Kiana climbed the stairs from the bottom floor.

Kiana pulled the phone from her ear and shook her head at him as if frustrated. "Haddie, if you're sure he's coerced, then you need to get out of Eugene."

Aaron sat at the kitchen counter on one of the high, wire-backed chairs. *Once again,* he thought. He closed his laptop and swiveled to hear what trouble Haddie had gotten herself into.

Kiana had her black hair braided with colorful beads so that it hung down one side of her brown face. Her lips were pursed and tight as she crossed with a quick pace to the living room. He and Kiana both left the curtains pulled closed, but the summer sun squeezed around the edges and provided plenty of light. The only real sign that they occupied the house was the old truck out front and the whirring air conditioner in the back. He had grown comfortable with the house, more so after learning some of the secrets that Thomas and Haddie kept. People were less likely to risk his exposure if it might mean their own. At least, he believed it would hold true of Thomas. Haddie proved to be a constant wildcard. She had the local detective calling her every other day, looking for Thomas.

The last couple of weeks had been awkward, as he blamed Boise on Kiana. If they had not been meeting with an investigator, then they likely would not have been exposed. The network Thomas had put together still would have burned, but they would not have been attacked. The small smear of demon cells he'd gotten during the fight had proved they were mutated humans, but little else. It had hardly been worth the disaster that followed.

Kiana had not understood his tension. In fact, she had said that he could not blame her for the danger, but that was not the whole of his concerns. When he had run out of bullets, his instinct had nearly caused him to use his power. That terrified him. The nightmares and the guilt had ridden him throughout college like the weight of Atlas. He could not live with that again. How Haddie and her father managed to deal with it was impossible for him to fathom. Haddie showed her regrets and pain. Thomas seemed as cold as stone.

"Let me ask him," Kiana said.

Aaron tried not to show that he took a sharp breath in. *I am not getting involved.* He kept his face emotionless as she pulled the phone down.

Kiana sighed and faced him. "Haddie's coworker, a man named Josh, has been coerced. Obviously, she's concerned about the implications that they may be after her, but it is possible they are merely looking for information on Harold Holmes."

Aaron ran his finger along the bridge of his nose. A lifetime of glasses and only a year of contacts left him with the habit of repositioning his frames. He had difficulty resisting the lingering mannerism when he found himself concerned. Haddie had been revealed. If someone coerced her, then his location would be quickly compromised. He would have to start looking at plans to move on, possibly tonight. Too many people knew of his whereabouts.

"She wants to know if you could think of any way to remove it?" Kiana addressed the comment innocently.

A cold rush of dread flowed down the back of his head. Anger flushed his cheeks. Haddie should have approached him discretely. *Alone.* He still would have denied her implication of any possibility for him to use his powers; that would not be an option. Would she expose his secret?

Aaron swallowed. "No idea."

Thomas, Haddie, and Kiana tended to jump in with little thought. This coerced coworker could be a ploy to expose Haddie. Had it worked? *I need to get out of here before this all goes up in flames.*

Kiana paced in the living room, listening to Haddie who had obviously heard his comment. "Okay, then we'll see you in a few minutes."

Aaron's chest tightened. *She could be leading them here.* "She's coming here? Is that wise?"

"Too late." Kiana held up the phone. "I know her tone, and there was no talking her out of it. She says she'll be careful."

Careful and Haddie hardly mixed. "This is a bad idea. We should leave. How long before she gets here?"

Kiana shrugged. "Fifteen. Start walking if you want. This is one of the best leads we have." She put her phone on the counter and headed for the coffee pot.

This was a disaster, not a lead. What could they possibly learn about the Unceasing or whoever created demons from this coerced coworker? All it told them was that someone was zeroing in on Haddie, probably because of Boise. "How is this a lead?" he asked.

"If," Kiana paused letting the word hang as she ran water, "Haddie is not the target, then we have a chance to find out what they are looking for. We can trace this coworker's movements and see if they lead somewhere. Even back-trace his timeline, see who intersected with him. The closer we get to why and who, the better."

"If," Aaron agreed. There were possibilities, but he could barely breathe or think as he fought the urge to pack and run. He could wait this out and risk that the situation was not as dire as he feared, or react and leave before Haddie arrived. *I hate reacting.*

He unplugged his laptop and slid off the chair. "I am going for a walk. I need to think."

CHAPTER 5

Haddie pulled the RAV4 to the stoplight, waiting for Terry to answer his phone. The drive had taken some of the edge off, despite the traffic and the one driver who had blown his horn when she'd left the office distracted. The savory scents of Chinese takeout had her salivating.

Getting out of the office had allowed her brain to think through some of the implications to Josh's condition. She'd been running herself in circles trying to think her way through this. Dad and Sam had still not answered her messages. *They're fine, just busy.* Kiana, as expected, had cautioned Haddie, and seemed willing to get together to make plans. She seemed to think Josh's state was a benefit to them.

She'd calmed somewhat and could look at Josh's situation with empathy rather than fear. Who would do this to him, and why? Whether this was about Harold Holmes or Haddie herself didn't matter; she'd brought this on Josh. *I've got to fix this.* She'd killed coerced before, and worked through the guilt enough to live with it. An innocent coworker or friend would be entirely different.

Terry texted as the light turned green. Haddie hung up her call as she drove and glanced down to read his text. "I'll call back. Fifteen minutes." They all used burners since Boise. Liz had been excited to get one, saying that she felt like a real spy. Everything had changed after Dad had gone into hiding. Terry had scrubbed old texts and emails with the help of his less reputable friends. Everyone had settled into a new normal, until Josh. She watched behind her to see which cars also turned at the light; at her next turn, none followed.

Dad was letting Kiana and Aaron stay at a hillside house he owned under another name. The winding roads up there helped ease her stress. The few cars that drove along the farms and houses moved at an easy pace, and the summer's green fields helped calm her.

The steep driveway seemed to swallow her as if she entered a different world away from the city. Pines and short oaks crawled up the hill, and the field ranged from green to browning tan. The old Ford truck was parked out front. Little else about the house gave any indication that anyone was staying there. The birds' chirping and the buzz of insects surrounded her as she exited with the takeout and walked to the house.

Haddie knocked before trying the door and finding it open. They kept the house dark, forcing her eyes to adjust.

Kiana had brewed fragrant coffee and sat at the counter with a black mug. A tense smile came to her lips. "You okay?"

Haddie shrugged and moved for the counter. "Not really, but better." Her throat thickened and she focused on unpacking the food and gathering plates. She jumped when Kiana put her hand on her shoulder. The woman didn't say anything, but Haddie nearly came to tears. "It's my fault. Josh would be okay if it weren't for me — for Harold Holmes, the raves, Boise — all of it."

"Perhaps, but letting them continue wouldn't have been the right thing to do. Whoever is able to coerce people is at fault, not you."

Haddie motioned toward the takeout and scanned the dark room again. "Where's Aaron?"

Kiana sniffed. "Probably out in the bushes watching the driveway. He's got it in his head that this is a trap. You know how he is."

"To see if I was followed?" Haddie raised her eyebrows. "I was careful."

Her burner rang and she put Terry on speaker. "Hi, Terry. I've got you on speaker with Kiana."

"Hey, Special K. Where's Doc?" Terry asked.

"Hiding in a bush." Haddie laid the phone on the counter and started serving herself lunch. "I've got a problem, and it could affect all of us. Josh showed back up to work today, and he's been coerced."

"No way. The yellow face thing?"

"Yep." Haddie stabbed a piece of broccoli, enjoying the salty sauce.

"You didn't . . ."

"Terry. No." She choked. "He didn't attack. He just went on his computer. I peeked once and saw him looking at emails."

"Yours?"

"Didn't get that close." She took another bite as the door opened and Aaron stepped inside.

"What's he after — rather — what are they after?" Terry asked. "We know these people are interconnected, but are they an organization? Someplace out of India where the holding company is? Sameedha and Anthony's funds went there, and the Unceasing seem to use their facilities, along with this Lady Erica the fashion designer. My money is that the Unceasing are behind this, or whoever runs that. They've been radicalizing against tech companies and national governments in their posts. Doomsday prep is their biggest focus now, they've got classes in New Mexico and Texas on how to survive the coming apocalypse. Your coerced friend has to be tied to the leader of the Unceasing."

Kiana passed Aaron, bringing a plate of Chinese food to the counter. "Exactly. We need to use this. Can you track what he's doing at the law firm? The emails he's looking at? Maybe we can figure out who if we know what he's looking for. It could be Haddie, or it could be something else. But I think if they wanted Haddie directly, they would have moved by now. Hopefully, they don't know about her."

"Haddie can give me remote access, but their IT might be alerted. I can't know until we get in there," Terry said. "It would be a risk. You'd have to have a story ready."

Haddie ate fried rice and watched Aaron. Tall with a strong nose and dirty blond hair, he could be considered handsome. He walked around them both and took his seat at the end of the counter, leaning against the wall. As usual with their discussions, he looked as though he disapproved.

She put her fork down. "What do you think, Aaron?"

Aaron shrugged and looked at Kiana. "If you and Terry want to put yourselves at risk, then so be it. Don't involve me in this. I am not inclined."

"Didn't you want to go to New York and search the Unceasing office?" Haddie asked.

He shrugged. "I didn't intend to break in and stomp around like we did at Boise. That was Kiana."

"So, what do you think we should do?"

"We?" he asked. "I am willing to observe. This wild conjecture you've come up with isn't going to be true just because you want it to be. You can stir up the beehive and I will watch what comes flying out." Aaron had almost a smug look as he said the latter part.

"You're a coward." Haddie clenched her jaw and shook her head. He wasn't helping. Why did she think he would? He did fine on the conspiracy forums, but she'd saved his ass twice when he came out from behind his computer.

Kiana raised her hand, as if trying to calm their conversation. "I think Aaron is being practical. We should limit contact, but observe this coworker of yours. Maybe your father could help us set up someone to watch his residence. Tapping his phones and monitoring his computers would be optimal. He should have to report in to his handler."

Aaron nodded. "Have someone else take the risk. If I were you, I would not be going back to work. But, I doubt you can resist."

Haddie's face flushed. "Josh is someone I know. He's likely in this trouble because of me. I can't just discard him. I need to fix him."

"And how do you intend to do that?"

She almost blurted out his secret.

He saw it in her eyes and his finger rubbed the bridge of his nose. His lip tightened, and they locked eyes for a moment. Almost imperceptibly, he shook his head slowly.

I can't expect any help from Aaron. He had the coercion power and had used it once in college. If anyone had a chance to fix Josh, it was Aaron, but he wouldn't. She had to find another way. Haddie stuffed another forkful of Chinese food into her mouth and glared at her plate. *I need to find who did this.* Force them to fix it.

She swallowed her food, no longer hungry. "Terry, what do I need to do to give you access?"

PART 2

Technology, greed, and war have become gods here.

"Mistress."

Her attendants paused their painting of her skin, and she turned her head slightly. "What is it, Tyrone?"

"A message."

I don't need to ask who. The only messages that came through the tablet were from the General. Hopefully, he didn't intend to change his directives again. The trip through Eugene had caused her to compact her schedule even tighter so that it had been a rush to get to the Governor in time for the dinner last night. Today, she had a rare moment of personal time before she met with a group of investors. The General had targeted one particular man, thus forcing her to use her powers one night after the next. It drained her.

She didn't share his fanaticism or even vision, but she didn't dare try to run or disappoint him. As generous with praise as he could be, he could be merciless to those who failed him. Sameedha had come into line eventually, before she'd died in that horrendous fire at one of her raves. *I still don't believe that was an accident.* Especially not since Barbara last month. Someone, or some group had been working against the General.

Tyrone waited near the door of the lavish Californian hotel suite. Her attendants had cleared the furniture from the main sitting room, leaving only a tile floor, which made the space expansive. Short and dark haired with her mark glowing on his face, held her tablet so it faced her, waiting. She gestured and he stepped forward, clicked on the message, and squarely faced the tablet toward her.

The General had written two lines. "Congratulations on the Governor. Have your target call me tonight, afterward."

After I turn the man. She nodded to Tyrone who took the tablet away. Her two attendants, a young blond male just out of high school and a larger muscled man, continued painting her skin white. There was no need to reply to the General. He'd not offered a question, merely congratulated her on bringing the Governor into her control and confirming her next target.

The Governor had been easy, happy to be alone with her for a few minutes. Her ability always disoriented the subject for a varying length of time; she needed a short period with them immediately afterward. The initial disturbance lasted longer. Her pets could be unpredictable for hours, even days. She'd suggested to him that he blame eating bad oysters, as the dish had been his suggestion. *I hate seafood.*

The investor tonight would be more difficult with such a crowd — but perhaps not — males were easy to manipulate. He would be trapped, as she was.

Her attendants had reached her feet and she hadn't noticed until one spoke. "Mistress."

She lifted her foot so they could paint the sole. Today's activities would be a minor distraction, a treat that she grasped while she could. This evening and the two days following would be exhausting. *I deserve to be pampered for a couple hours.*

When they had finished painting her, only her red pubic hair retained any color. From her shaved head to her toes, she glistened titanium white. They began dressing her as Tyrone waited, seeming to stare through her and out the windows to the city far below. After they laced her into a latex bodysuit, Tyrone stepped forward to do her makeup. He was the only one she trusted to do it right.

One of the attendants gathered the paints and brushes and scurried into one of the bedrooms. The other remained, holding the makeup kit for Tyrone. Proper, and in control, she caught a glint of some agency over her life. Imprisoned in a perpetual twenty-three year old body and cornered into the General's crusade, there were rare moments over the past decade when her life felt like her own. It hadn't started this way.

"I am finished, Mistress." Tyrone remained as the final attendant disappeared.

"Very well, have them enter."

He retreated into another bedroom, and within moments, a couple began crawling across the tile toward her. Tyrone followed with her equipment.

An older man in his late twenties had long brown hair, a muscular physique, and wore the harness well. The woman had been fitted into a latex catsuit so that little of her showed except her form.

Tyrone held a paddle, a whip, and a baton. "Mistress?"

The day's pressures drifted away. *I deserve this.* She smiled at the two kneeling on the tile. Her submissives were volunteers. There was no pleasure in dominating someone she controlled.

CHAPTER 7

Just east of Bend, Thomas pulled into the driveway of the front property where he'd set up the dog kennel. The land connected to a farm he'd bought, where he had set up their home. The dirt road just past the business cut through thin pine forests to a large acreage where they had once grown spinach. The green Gator four-wheeler was parked by the office door. Sam and Meg would be with the two dogs they boarded. The house turned into a business and the farm hidden behind had served as a discreet location to start a new identity. Dirt roads wound through both properties, leaving him plenty of exits. He had to be concerned that the writer of the letter might have gotten closer than just his drop box in Creswell. *I'll have to burn all my active phones, just in case.* Phone service proved sketchy at best, while nearer to the farm they had almost no reception.

At the end of the drive, he pulled behind a steel barn onto a cement slab and turned off his bike. Pine and dogs mixed with the smell of the hot engine. The concrete pad had once held an RV, based on the position of the electric, water, and sewage connections. The area around the barn still had swaths of rusty dirt where the previous owner had left broken-down trucks. Sam would likely meet him here. She'd frantically texted and called during his trip, and she couldn't miss his bike pulling into the yard. Wincing, he climbed off, removed his helmet, and smoothed his hair back.

"Where have you been?" Sam, wearing her best frown and a pink and blue T-shirt, appeared around the corner of the barn. Shoulder length black hair flopped over her shoulders as she came to a stop and put her hands on her hips.

Thomas couldn't help but smile. He'd never seen her mad before, but he couldn't blame her. "I couldn't call." He wouldn't tell her about the letter, which wasn't completely fair because she was at risk and didn't know it, but he wasn't about to explain any more than she already knew. "I'm afraid the number's been compromised. We'll set you up with a new phone as well. Consider your old one burnt."

Sam's mouth dropped open, and her hands jumped to her face. "FBI? Police?"

"Can't be sure." He pulled out his water bottle and rattled it. The still heat felt like it sucked the oxygen out of the air. "Let's get inside. Meg?"

"Playing with Louis and Bandit on the porch." She pursed her lips. "We're okay?"

"I'm pretty sure. Just being careful. I'm more concerned about Haddie." He motioned toward the front of the barn. Air warped off the metal. "Let me get something to drink, and we'll contact her. Did you reply to her?"

Sam tucked her hands behind her back as they walked. "No, I didn't want her to get even more upset since I couldn't get a hold of you."

He nodded. "Good."

They walked across the drive toward the front of the old

white house. The single story had been added onto enough that it spread out the back to a fence that connected to the barn. He'd been able to remodel inside and out to board a good number of dogs. The will for his present identity named Sam to inherit the properties, though she didn't know it. If he needed to disappear again, she deserved it for the risk she took. Besides, if something did happen to him, she'd take care of Meg. He'd survived wounds he shouldn't have, but just barely. He didn't have any delusions of being invulnerable.

Sam led the way into the house. Cool air drifted through the open door. He'd turned the living room into an office with a gated reception area and tile floors; sometimes pups got nervous in a new place. Over the scent of the dogs, he could smell a spicy dish, possibly rice from their lunch. Thomas headed into the kitchen, poured himself some water, and drank as he reached into the cabinet over the fridge. Behind the bags of coffee, he found a fresh burner phone.

"You keep one here?" Sam seemed surprised.

Thomas tilted his head. "You never know." Filling his cup, he headed back out to the reception area and plugged in a charger. "You know how to pull the battery out of your old phone? I have a new one for you at the house." He had a dozen.

Sam nodded quickly and dug into her pocket.

He turned on the new phone and waited. It had almost fifty percent power. He navigated to a game site and opened up the chat; there were only two friends, Jerk and Whitey. He messaged them both. "Consider any number connected to my old number burnt. Same for anyone you ever connected to, and anyone they connected to." Haddie's links included Kiana, so he'd have to get that new number.

Hopefully the web of connections would end with Haddie's friends. He typed in his new phone number.

I hope Haddie's being smart. Someone coercing a coworker was dangerous. She'd probably been fretting over it and wanted to fix the poor soul. He drew a deep breath and finished his water. Leaving the phone on the charger, he headed toward the back porch where he could hear Louis yapping.

The air on the porch was hot despite the shade and two ceiling fans. Louis bounced to him and placed his paws on his knee. Bandit, the boarded gray terrier, followed behind.

Meg sat on the floor with a knotted tug toy, smiling through a mop of auburn hair. "Hey, T. Sam's been worried. I told her you were okay."

"I am. What did you two do this morning?" He reached down to pat the two heads at his knees.

Meg tossed her hair, waving the toy at the dogs, though they didn't leave him. "We walked the dogs. The angels were out this morning."

He glanced at Sam, who looked awkward. This was the second comment from Meg of this sort. *Is this her coping?* She seemed to be adapting well to their new lifestyle. He'd planned on homeschooling her this fall, but perhaps she needed more social interaction than him, Sam, and the dogs. *Let's see where this goes.*

Thomas sat in one of the wicker chairs and the dogs returned to Meg. Sam joined her on the floor. The letter still burned in his inside pocket. This author knew too much about him.

He'd have to wait for Haddie's response. She'd get a phone and call him soon; hopefully she'd left the office. Kiana at least had a calm head about these things. *Do I risk going to Eugene myself?* Haddie needed to disappear.

Haddie pulled her RAV4 into the intersection and waited for a lawn crew with a trailer to amble past before she took a right turn. Her regular cell vibrated with a message.

She grimaced, catching Grace's name with a glance. *I'm going to be so late.* It was well past one in the afternoon. Discussing the situation with the others had taken longer than she expected, but she hadn't really been considering the time. Josh had her freaked out. Part of her screamed at the idea of heading back to the firm. *I have to.*

Dad's message on the gaming system had kicked her into motion. She'd warned Kiana and Aaron before taking off and promised to pick them up a couple phones as well. Traffic seemed to snarl under the heat, and the pavement wavered between cars. Her own car had smelled like a dryer when she first got in. The AC barely seemed more than a cool breeze.

What had spooked Dad? It wasn't Josh.

Haddie turned into the store's parking lot and searched for the ATM. She'd need cash for the purchase. Driving down the lane between parked cars, she watched the road behind her to see if anyone followed. Each turn on the way here, she'd cataloged the cars and made sure none shadowed her.

She slammed on the brakes instinctively as a car finished backing from a parking space. Her cell and water bottle flew to the passenger floor with a clatter. The driver stopped and beeped, probably seeing how close she'd come. Taking a moment to roll down their window, they gave her the finger before continuing forward. *Pay attention, Haddie.* She took their parking spot and sat for a moment.

Ten minutes later, standing in line at the counter buying three pre-paid phones and cards with cash, she felt sure that everyone watched and judged. The flushed boy ringing her up didn't say a word but glanced up at her each time he scanned an item. The older man putting pants and chips on the belt behind her smiled when she turned. She didn't have time to go to three different stores, but everyone noticed what she was doing. *I am horrible at this.*

She shook by the time she reached the RAV4, opened her pre-paid phone, and plugged it into the charger. She had worked out a plan with Terry to send him her new number in pieces. He loved the intrigue and conspiracy and would likely already have his new burner phone. She sent Terry three sets of numbers with her regular cell via text, message, and email, disguising them in the conversation he'd suggested. He responded immediately on each one. *He was just waiting for this.*

Pulling out the Chinese menu with Dad's new number written on it, she dialed.

"Hey," he answered. "This your new number?"

"Yes." Haddie cleared her throat, wishing she'd filled her water before leaving. "What happened, Dad?"

"First, Josh. You're not at work, are you?"

Haddie shook her head, staring out over the heat rising off the parking lot. "Not yet; I'm going back now." She needed to sit a moment before driving.

"Don't. It's not worth it, Haddie. I'd suggest grabbing Rock and disappearing with us, but I know you won't. Just don't go back to work. Find a new job."

"We've got a plan."

"I don't like it."

Haddie raised her eyebrows. "You haven't even heard it."

"Does it involve you going back to the law firm and this coerced coworker?"

"Josh — and yes."

"I don't like it."

Haddie took a deep breath. "Terry needs me to give him remote access. He'll hack in and see what Josh is up to."

Dad didn't answer immediately. "I don't like it." He sighed loudly. "That won't stop you though. I'm tempted to come to Eugene, but I'm concerned I'd bring trouble with me. The police, at least, will still be expecting that."

Haddie selfishly wished he could come to Eugene. Not that she couldn't deal with this on her own, Dad just made her feel safer and she could count on him. *I can't have him come.* "What happened today? Why burn the phones?"

"I got a letter today in one of my drop boxes. Only two people know the box, and one went missing in Boise. They know a little of my previous identity — Meg's family. I can't take a chance that they've been tracking for a while and picked up on my phones. I had to start fresh on everything, just in case." A dog barked in the background. "I'll show it to you. Let's meet tomorrow. I've compared some of the rhetoric to the Unceasing website, and I think they're connected."

"What does the letter say? What did they want?"

"They want me to join them."

Haddie nearly dropped her phone. Her heart already raced a bit from buying the phones, and her hands shook. "What?"

"I'll show you. Makes me wonder about Harold Holmes and his brother, and why there's an interest in them."

Haddie twisted her white hair into a knot at her shoulder. The Unceasing were trying to recruit Dad. Surely he wouldn't do it, but what were they trying to do? This wasn't just about getting money from the raves. There had to be a bigger purpose than that. What had Barbara's function been in all this? She wanted to read the letter. "Where do you want to meet? At your place?"

"No, but I'll bring Sam and Meg. Let me work on a meeting place." He cleared his throat. "You need to disappear Haddie, come join us. We'll dye your hair."

I can't leave everyone. Just his mention of it made her chest feel hollow. "I can't. Won't. Not yet."

"You're risking your friends."

"Don't put that on me, Dad." She stiffened. "I need to go. Already an hour late from lunch. Terry's waiting on me." His instructions were on the back side of the menu.

"Be careful. I love you."

"I will. Love you too, Dad." Haddie hung up and held the phone in her fist. He was probably right. She might just be risking everyone by going back to the law firm. Aaron believed that she was. However, if the coerced Josh looked for information on Harold Holmes, first he'd find nothing; second, he might just lead Terry to whomever was looking for people like her and her dad. *Isn't that worth it?* She took a deep breath and put the RAV4 into reverse.

Josh was their best chance.

I'm using him. She flushed at the thought. He hadn't asked for this. No one considered how to fix him, except Liz. Haddie would have to approach Dad on that later. Kiana might not want him un-coerced. *I can't leave him like that. Once we get some information, we'll try Liz's idea.*

Taking a deep breath, Haddie headed back to work.

CHAPTER 9

Haddie stepped into the office and smelled barbecue. *Toby.* She liked a strange, pungent, barbecued tofu from one of the nearby restaurants.

Toby looked up from her desk and quickly gestured toward the kitchen. She jumped up, fluttering a short green and white skirt, and disappeared into the hall behind her. Flashing past the entrance on the far wall, Toby headed toward the kitchen.

Fresh coffee sat in the pot and the counters looked spotless as usual. Haddie had rushed out of the hill house, leaving a mess for Kiana and Aaron.

"Something's wrong with Josh," Toby whispered.

Haddie swallowed. "He seemed a little off."

"That's it, he's almost normal. Andrea has me trying to contact his mother, but she's not answering." Toby tilted her head and leaned forward, letting brown locks slide off her shoulders. "Andrea is going to go by there before we close. Josh is in the copy room and says he'll stay as late as it takes to get the scanning done. He hasn't eaten."

Josh ate regularly, and usually in large quantities. He'd

covered his desk in takeout many times. Did the coercion override everything? What had happened to his mother? She was sick, but Haddie didn't know much more.

"Grace tried to sit him down and talk, but he just blew it off and said he was catching up." Toby shrugged. "We don't know what to do."

If Josh were scanning, this might be the best time to get Terry in. Those three boxes might take until everyone left for the night, leaving Josh free with the computers. Probably what he planned, or had been told to do. *Is there any of him left?* Could anything fix him? Haddie squirmed but responded because Toby expected it. "Maybe he'll be back to normal, or not normal, by Monday. We should let him be. He might be working through something that happened to him while he was gone." Josh had been absent since before Boise; no one had been able to get much from Andrea. "Do we know what happened while he was gone?"

Toby shook her head. "Andrea didn't say. I only asked once."

"Then we should cut him some slack. Who knows what he's been going through." Haddie almost shivered. What did the coerced experience? Did they remember everything? Did they have their own wants and needs? Haddie started making tea, pulling out the warming coffee to brew hot water.

Toby didn't press the point, but stood thoughtfully. "I tried to get him to eat. Offered to run for something since he was busy."

"Did you try bagels?" Haddie smiled.

Toby returned the weak smile. "No. Might be a good idea. I've never seen him resist a bagel." Her expression darkening quickly, she turned and headed back down the hall.

Once Haddie had set her tea aside to brew, she followed. Her glass lay in her cubicle. As she passed the office door, Andrea nodded Haddie inside. Her stomach roiled as she shifted mid-step and turned into the office. *I should have at least called.*

Andrea sat at her desk cluttered with papers and gestured Haddie closer. Her hair had loosened, leaving bright red strands to escape the bun held by two dragon-headed hair sticks. "Have you talked with Josh?" She spoke quietly, but not quite at a whisper.

Haddie shook her head. This was not about being late. "Is he going to be okay?" She'd said that to deflect her knowledge — and perhaps to distract from being late.

"I don't know. See if you can get him talking."

That wasn't happening. "Okay." Haddie nodded enthusiastically and offered a smile. She turned to leave when Andrea focused on her monitor.

"Oh, and let us know when you're taking an extended lunch."

Haddie swallowed. "Yes. Sorry."

She slunk into the back office, catching a glance from Grace. The scanner in the copy room whirred. Josh stood out of sight, but she could see his glow through the wall, motionless. Relieved, she grabbed her glass and turned toward the opening to the hall, partially tempted to skip the tea for the moment rather than wander past Andrea's door.

"You okay?" Grace asked. Her voice seemed quieter than usual, and she didn't stop typing.

Haddie nodded. "I guess. You?"

"Concerned."

"Me too." Glass in hand, Haddie thought of the instructions in her back pocket and felt her pulse quicken. *I'm procrastinating.*

Taking a deep breath, she started for the kitchen with quick, decisive steps. *Some tea and hacking.* Using Josh like this made her queasy, but she would discuss Liz's idea with Dad tomorrow when they met. She would at least try to push this coercion out of him, even if it failed. If she thought there was any chance, she'd work on Aaron and get him to try. The only other option she could imagine involved whoever did this in the first place — and Terry's hack might lead them to that person. There might be some rationalization in her logic, but she couldn't think of a better option.

The tea swirled hot and cold in her palm when she returned. Josh dropped one of the boxes on the other side of Haddie's cubicle and she nearly froze in the hall. The flourescent lighting diffused some of the glow and she could make out a smile and nod.

Tense and filled with false cheer, she offered a greeting for Andrea's sake. "How's it going, Josh? Sorry I hadn't got to some of that yet."

"Don't worry, I'll get through it today." He strode over to the remaining two boxes beside his cubicle, looking disturbingly odd in both his gait and being dressed in professional clothes.

Haddie shivered as she sat down and tested a sip of earthy tea with her hand trembling. *I've got to fix this.* Following Terry's instructions, she texted him the information prompted by her computer. He sent back a quick thumbs up and she waited stiffly with ears burning and glancing between her cubicle wall on Grace's side and the hallway entrance. Nervous, she stood and moved some folios onto a stack at the back of her cubicle. Part of her waited for sirens to sound from the IT closet in the back of the copy room where Josh worked, or Andrea's phone to ring with an alert. Nothing happened, except she earned a quizzical glance from Grace.

Terry texted, and Haddie jumped for her phone. "First thing I did when I got into the server was check the logs. Somebody in your office let in an outside connection already. I'm out. I'm bouncing out of Singapore, but it wouldn't take long for someone sophisticated to find me. Sorry, Buckaroo."

Haddie barely managed to type, "Okay."

Josh had let someone into Andrea's network. *I can't warn her. What would I tell her?*

Terry texted back, "I'm going to try and trace this. Not directly. I've got a couple people who are better protected that will help."

Haddie stared at her monitor, wanting to embrace the idea and find some hope in it. *It means letting Andrea get hacked.* Josh or Andrea — not really a choice. Whoever Josh had let in would likely be looking for information about Harold Holmes. *Or me.* That wouldn't affect Andrea's clients. Still, it felt like a betrayal.

"Okay," Haddie typed. A miserable choice.

HADDIE PULLED her RAV4 into the parking space under the overhang of her apartment building. Thick, unyielding air enclosed her when she stepped out. She paused and tried to exhale some of the tense frustration she felt from the day. In the next parking space, her Fatboy gathered dust during the summer heat. As she walked around it and toward the stairs, a rich, earthy aroma of hot grass mixed with a floral scent from one of the wilted flowering shrubs. They needed rain.

Rock greeted her at the door and stuck his black, pit bull muzzle into her hand. Her new dog walker, a red-headed college student named Roslyn, came by twice during the days that Haddie worked. Rock seemed to miss Sam as much as Haddie did; he tended to be needy when she got home.

"Give me a minute, Boy. We'll take a good walk." Haddie tossed her purse on her computer chair.

To her left, Jisoo screamed from the kitchen. Roslyn had surely fed her, but the calico wouldn't let up until a new course had been served. Haddie annoyed the cat as she took a moment to plug in her new burner; it had dropped below a ten percent charge. Cringing, she ran some water in the cereal bowl she'd left in the sink. Jisoo had left a spatter of dried milk from her foray into the leftovers.

"I've got you, Jisoo." The calico balanced along the edge of the counter and bumped Haddie's elbow.

Once she'd gotten Jisoo fed and Rock outside, Haddie felt more normal than she had for most of the day since Josh showed up coerced. When she'd left work, she walked to the parking lot with Toby, leaving Josh and Grace inside. Guilt over the ongoing hack and leaving Grace alone with a coerced had left Haddie panicked and frustrated. The drive home through rush hour traffic didn't help. Who had done this to Josh? *I have to remember to text Grace — make sure she's okay.*

Liz hadn't called or texted in the afternoon like she often did. She'd been warned to get a new burner, but they often talked on their regular cells. Sick, she probably went straight to bed after work. Haddie wouldn't call, though Liz and Sam tended to help her get through the rougher decisions.

David had been the only bright point in Haddie's day. She couldn't enjoy it though, with everything else in a mess.

Haddie planned on dinner at the hillside house. She'd left the extra pre-paid phones in her car; Kiana and Aaron would need them, and Haddie wanted another round of discussion. There had to be another plan other than just waiting while Andrea got hacked. *How can I get Aaron to help?* He wouldn't.

Rock walked her down the road beside Sam's old apartment. It would be good to see her tomorrow. She'd have a new number too. No wonder she hadn't responded. Haddie sighed, leading them back toward her apartment. *I need my friends*. Dad still hadn't set a place and time for their meet; the letter had him spooked. If it had been one of his investigators who talked, how much had they known?

Haddie reached the steps to her apartment. How long would she wait for Terry to trace the hack? Aaron possessed the one skill that had the best chance to fix Josh. He wouldn't need to do it alone. Haddie and Kiana could be there to protect him. What did he have to lose? She stomped up the last couple of steps. *I have to try and persuade him.* She'd bring them fish for dinner and be polite. She closed her eyes, trying to remember what he ordered for meals on the way to Boise. Where did they sell Moosehead lager in Eugene?

As Haddie stepped in the hillside house, she juggled a to-go order and a shopping bag with clinking bottles and rattling cell phone packages. She offered a broad smile for Aaron, who sulked in his usual spot at the counter by the wall. He closed his laptop as she entered, but didn't return the smile.

The AC felt good as she stepped into the kitchen. None of the usual breeze came from the north. The shadows were long outside, but even the dwindling sun and shade didn't drive away the heat.

Kiana got up from the couch and moved across the living room. "So why the burn? What did Thomas find out?"

Haddie drew a tight breath. "One of his investigators is missing from Boise." She wouldn't tell them about the letter. It involved questions that would be difficult to answer.

Aaron just watched, but Kiana nodded and said, "He thinks they might have accessed a phone with his information."

Haddie guessed that the man had been alive and either interrogated or coerced. Dad had said they communicated via a gaming app, similar to the one she used with him. In his usual abundance of caution, he had decided the phones could be a risk. Any version brought them to the same conclusion: the old burners had to go.

Kiana accepted the answer and sniffed the air as she got into the kitchen. "Any word from Terry?"

Haddie shook her head. "I told him that I was coming over here. He asked that we call when we get done with dinner. Fish good? I went to Fisherman's Market."

Kiana shrugged. "Hard to imagine fresh fish when you can't smell the ocean, but I'm hungry."

Haddie had gotten aromatic swordfish, salmon tacos, and a crab mac'n'cheese that they would attempt to share. Tacos may have been a bad plan to split. Aaron had grudgingly taken his lager, but seemed wary at the offer.

Kiana ignored his sullen mood as she tasted each item. "This is great. Well, it's not from Louisiana, but it's better than I expected." She sat at the opposite end of the counter from Aaron. "Can I get your dad's number from you?"

"He asked me to give it to you." *What did they talk about? He never talked with Aaron. Hell, I rarely do either.*

"Aaron, do you think Terry's friends will get us something? I'm not up on this tech stuff." She sipped at her Two Hearted Ale, waiting for him to respond.

He paused with a piece of swordfish on his fork. "I think that depends on their skills — which I know nothing about." Popping the fish in his mouth, he focused on his food.

The rest of the meal, Haddie couldn't get Aaron to engage. He seemed more withdrawn than usual. Perhaps he was leaving. *I've still got to try.* She just needed a moment alone with him.

After dinner while they set up their phones, Haddie called Terry.

He answered immediately. "Hey, Buckaroo. Everybody there? Doc? Special K?"

Kiana smirked. "We're here."

"Did you know Lady Erica is doing a fashion show in northern California? We should go."

"Might need an invite, depends on what kind of event." Kiana tugged on her earlobe. "Why?"

"She's definitely involved, but we know that. What I'm thinking is to have Haddie go down with her special vision, see if all the models are coerced. Boom. Then we know she's got that power."

Haddie raised her eyebrows. It wasn't a bad idea. "When is it?"

"Sunday. San Francisco."

A drive of eight or nine hours, if she remembered correctly. What did she have going on Sunday? *Not Liz.* Dad was tomorrow.

Kiana leaned toward the phone. "Why do you assume that she would coerce her models?"

"I would," Terry responded. "But at least some of them, or her staff should be at least."

"So were Sameedha's and Barbara's — at least the guards." *I still like the idea.* How could she force this woman to fix Josh? If she had the power.

"You don't have to do anything," Terry said. "Just check it out. She's going down to LA and then heads back east after that. It's just so close."

Aaron finally spoke, "It will be dangerous. Haddie is the only one who can protect herself from powers; not even

Thomas was able to do that, from what you described. I think it might be useful, but too risky for the rest of us."

Kiana shrugged. "I could go as backup. I don't need to get close."

"Me too," Terry said.

Aaron leaned against the wall. "Why Haddie needs moral support I do not know. If there is a well thought out plan, then I would go — to observe. I would rather wait until we get the results of the trace."

"Going to the fashion show won't affect Terry's friends. Besides, we might know something by then," Kiana said.

Haddie could sense a tension between him and Kiana. Aaron seemed to blame her for something since Boise, but he hadn't been injured or thrown back in time. What did he have to complain about?

Aaron shrugged without a response.

Kiana turned to Haddie. "That's four of us then. A tight fit in your SUV. What time is this event, Terry? We should get there early."

"Two in the afternoon." Terry sounded apologetic. "The hotel was owned by Anthony before he gave it over to Sameedha's rave companies. It's a formal thing. I've been looking it up as we're talking. You won't be able to get invites. Maybe Haddie can infiltrate as staff, steal a jacket or something. I'll text the address and a link to the event."

Kiana caught Haddie's eye and spoke quietly. "Thomas?"

The last thing Dad needed was something else to worry about. She'd love to have him along, but he had the letter to worry about. "I doubt it."

"Doubt what?" Aaron looked annoyed.

"That Dad would want to go," Haddie said.

"Would we fit?" asked Terry.

If they put Dad in the front passenger seat they would. Haddie shook her head. "He's got stuff to deal with."

"What?" asked Aaron. He watched her face.

Haddie pasted on a smile, but Aaron's constant suspicion wore on her. *He's not going to help Josh.* "The whole phone thing. He'll be fine. I just doubt he wants to get involved in anything else right now."

Kiana faced Haddie. "If we think this fashion designer is responsible for coercing people, what do *you* plan to do?"

The emphasis made Haddie pause. *What would I do? Kidnap her? Force her to fix Josh?* Then Haddie probably would have to go into hiding. *Unless I killed her.* She shook her head at her own thoughts. She wouldn't be killing anyone. Just investigate. And leave Josh coerced? "I don't know. We got time to think about it."

"We've got tomorrow," Kiana said with an emphasis on the date.

"So, are we doing a call tomorrow? I was going to use the school library tomorrow morning. I want to dig a bit deeper into these connections between Lady Erica and these Indian shell companies. Trying to stay off my network and I've got a proxy I can get to from the school. Later in the day, Livia and I are running to a bookstore in Portland. We'll be back in the evening."

Kiana looked at Haddie and said, "Dinner again tomorrow?"

"Sounds good, Special K." Terry sounded enthusiastic.

Kiana smiled and nodded toward the takeout containers. "I'm throwing that out, before it ruins a good meal."

"Later, Doc, Buckaroo." Terry hung up.

Haddie checked her phone and saw that Dad had texted during the call. "Odell Lake. 10am. Remember the restaurant and trail? Bring Rock or they'll be livid. We'll be on the trail. Come find us. Be careful."

She smiled. Sam had to be missing Rock. *Odell Lake.* Dad had taken her there a few times, usually as a staging area for longer hikes, but there was a trail by the shore. She texted with the phone in her lap. "Got it. See you then."

Kiana closed the door as she left. It only gave Haddie a minute or two. She twisted her hair with her right hand.

"Aaron. I need your help," she said quietly.

He stared at her without any decisive expression, waiting.

"I can't leave Josh like this. I've got to try something. What if you used your powers and tried to reverse, or nullify, whatever is influencing him?"

His expression didn't change. "No. I will not use that power." No emotion — no regret.

Haddie flushed, warming her cheeks. "He needs someone to help him."

"Find someone else. I will not do it."

She huffed and clenched her hair. "Why not? Are you afraid? We can protect you."

Aaron didn't reply, but continued to stare without any sign of emotion.

"You are a coward," she said, emphasizing each word a bit too loudly.

The doorknob turned and Haddie dropped her hair and closed her eyes. She'd failed, but had expected to. She only had two options left: Liz's plan where Haddie tried to push it out; and Terry's, which might end up in a kidnapping. Dad would have some logical thoughts, which might include sacrificing Josh. However, Sam might be able to help Haddie figure out how far she was willing to go to save Josh. They would have to speak hypothetically.

Kiana came in with a concerned look. She'd likely heard the end of the exchange.

We're going to San Fran. Haddie sighed. "I need some sleep. See you tomorrow." Before Kiana closed the door, she headed out.

CHAPTER 12

Aaron watched Haddie storm out of the house. Sometimes she acted immature, yet she could use her power without flinching. *I envy that.* The house still smelled like fish. She had bought dinner just to try and win him over, and beer as well. He could not use his power no matter how much she wanted him to.

He sympathized with her wanting to help her friend at work. She did not understand the terror it brought just considering opening up to that force. *She is right. I am a coward.*

"What was that about?" Kiana asked.

Aaron shrugged. "We disagree."

Kiana tilted her head in a nod, as if accepting that answer. She walked across the living room and sat down on the couch. "What do you think about these plans? Do you think we should be going to the fashion show?"

They had no real plan. Kiana had to know that. An FBI agent would have sat in meetings where they detailed contingencies. They would not just pile in a car and go, hoping for the best. "I will reserve my judgment until after the meeting tomorrow and we see what comes out of that discussion. It seems we are far from an actual plan."

Kiana frowned slightly. "I can agree with that."

Why have I stayed here? The danger of being discovered again grew while he lingered in Eugene. He'd been sloppy when this all started — when he'd seen his first demon. The creature had been slashing apart a body in the parking garage of the hotel where he'd been speaking on evolutionary biology for an annual conference. The gruesome form and the violence had shaken him, but once he'd survived, his scientific curiosity had exploded. His online searches had yielded similar descriptions and experiences before his investigations had caught the attention of someone and demons had found their way to his apartment.

He had escaped and run. It still seemed possible that the government had some part in this, but Kiana's description of the FBI's actions made it likely that a secret faction worked inside the framework. They had tracked his phones and money withdrawals, nearly trapping him a few times.

So, what am I waiting for?

He had found allies in some of the groups. Terry had been one of those. Haddie's use of an usual power gained his attention after the ski lift. He now doubted his initial hypothesis that the creation of the demons had led to other genetic experiments, ones which created people like himself and Haddie. Aaron followed her back to Eugene and learned of the friendship with Terry, who had never known of her abilities until recently. His own curiosity had led him back to her and Eugene two more times. She and her friends seemed the most likely group to dig up, or stumble into, some of the answers that had eluded him. Perhaps the risk had risen too high. She wanted him to expose himself to those visions. *I can't do that again.*

CHAPTER 13

Thomas drove the bulky Ford Transit through a forest where sometimes the pines rose so high on each side it seemed they were in a canyon. The summer had dried out the wood and grass to a kindling point. Louis and Meg played in the back while Sam sat quietly beside him in the passenger seat.

The traffic on 58 had increased over the years. More trucks, commuters, and RVs rolled up and down the hills of the highway. Here on the west end of the road, the pines rarely allowed the larger hills and mountain tops to show. He feared a time when the gas station towns would become larger and cut swaths through this forest. At some point, man had to realize where this would lead.

"We should be coming to the entrance soon, on the left." Sam had set herself as the navigator, though the roads were simple and he had no doubt about how to get there.

"Mm-hmm." He'd come out with Haddie a few times when she'd been younger. The earlier trips she had enjoyed, then it had become "boring." His first time had been over a hundred years ago when route 58 had been nothing more than a wagon trail leading into the Willamette Valley. It hadn't become an actual road until after he served in the first world war. Since then, he'd taken to riding it to get to the mountains to the east when he lived near Eugene.

"There's the sign!" Sam sounded excited. She turned between the seats to interrupt Meg in the back. Nature didn't intimidate her, and the farm suited her. "We're here."

"We've still got a short drive down this road," he said.

"Half a mile," Sam corrected.

Some days, the wind blew harsh across the lake, but this would not be one of those days. The only stir in the forest was his block-shaped van winding down the road. A pick-up truck passed going in the opposite direction, but no one had pulled off 58 behind them.

They'd have half an hour to wait for Haddie if she wasn't early or late; either was possible. He'd texted that morning to make sure she hadn't gotten so busy she forgot. Meg and Sam would enjoy the lodge lakeside, and they could burn a few minutes picking up something, though Sam had been careful to pack plenty to eat and drink for the drive and hike.

The letter seemed to burn inside his vest pocket. He'd put it back in its envelope and folded it carefully. Each time he read it made him tense. Haddie would not like it. The more he compared it with the writings of the Unceasing, he could see the same hand behind the words. He'd been right all along that this was a war. He was being recruited.

After a right-hand turn he pulled in front of the lodge and stopped the van. A couple sedans and trucks parked around the wooden block of a building. "Leash Louis for now; we'll see how he does when he gets out on the trail. Make sure everything you want is in your packs. Check your CamelBaks we can fill up here. If you want a soda or a snack, this is the place."

As Sam moved to the back, he called Haddie.

"Hey, Dad."

"Haddie!" Sam and Meg yelled from the back.

"Hi." Haddie sounded pleased. She'd lost part of his attention when Meg came into the picture, then she'd lost him and Sam completely when he had to go underground. He didn't doubt she grieved. Hopefully this trip would help with the process. Rock grumbled in the background.

"How far out?" he asked.

"I'll be there at ten."

"We'll probably be on the trail and then wait for you to catch up." He'd rather limit anyone spotting them all together. "Everything look clear?" He didn't need her bringing the police out to him.

"All clear. I'll take a lap through Shelter Cove, just to be sure."

"Good. Smart. See you soon." He sighed as he hung up and shut off the van. He'd rarely had to go through this when he transitioned from one identity to the next. That sense of being hunted brought him back to the wars he'd been involved in. This time was worse, as he'd dragged Haddie into it.

The letter added a whole new level to the situation. He didn't just have to deal with a petty authority, or even modern-day police. This man smelled of war.

Sam handed him his pack and water. "Thanks," he said. "Let's do this."

PART 3

We can return to our status as protectors and mentors of mankind.

CHAPTER 14

THROUGH THE PINES Haddie caught glimpses of the deep blue lake to her right. Rock sat in the passenger seat of the RAV4 watching the road ahead. Dad's voice had perked him up, or perhaps it had been Sam and Meg. With the sun ahead of her, his black fur made him nearly a silhouette against the forest and water.

Deceptively cool in the SUV, it looked like a good day to hike. *Too late in the summer.* In reality, it would hit the eighties. She'd gone with solid hiking boots, jean shorts, and a midriff tank. The scars on her legs and arms had healed well, but she could still see them. They brought memories she tried to forget.

They drove up an incline, and she squinted against the sun. Her phone rang and the RAV4 picked it up. *An unknown number.* Liz?

Haddie answered the call. "Hello?"

"Sorry. I just walked my sorry ass in and bought a phone. I would have called on the cell, but wanted to find out what happened." The connection stretched out a few syllables.

"Driving in the hills. I might lose you. How are you feeling?"

"Better. Had a fever last night, but it broke this morning." Liz paused. "What's going on with Josh? Did you try?"

Haddie's face warmed. She hadn't tried to push the coercion out of Josh, not without talking it over with Dad, and he'd likely guard against it. Worse, she used Josh's condition to try and find out who did this to him. "No. Not yet. I might try and get Kiana or Dad to help. I'm going to meet him now." She left off the tracking that Terry did.

"So, you'll get your father to help?"

Doubtful. "At least I'll get his input." Haddie sighed. "Josh let someone into Andrea's network. We think they're looking for something on Harold Holmes, not me. Terry has someone tracing them."

"Did you tell Andrea? No. Tracing them is a good idea. Do you think it's the FBI? Kiana always thought they were focused on H.H." The connection wavered, but held.

Liz had mentioned the FBI before, but they wouldn't be the same ones causing the coercion. Someone seemed to be orchestrating all of this. "I guess the FBI would have the technology." *I hope it's not them.* Getting a lead back to the FBI would bring them no closer to whomever coerced Josh. If it did, Terry's plan for the San Francisco show made even more sense. Perhaps he suspected the FBI as well. "Terry suggested we go to the fashion show that is connected to the Indian companies. It's tomorrow."

"When do you leave? I'm not going, I'd just get everyone sick."

"Tomorrow morning. Probably. We're going to talk tonight.

"If you blast any demons, get me a better sample. Aaron's smear was too degraded."

Haddie raised her eyebrows. "It's not going to go down like Boise."

"You're breaking up. Just be careful, okay?" Liz's words stretched and broke.

"I will. Get some rest."

"Count on it."

In a few minutes, Haddie pulled her RAV4 into the lodge parking lot and saw Dad's Ford Transit. When she stepped out, the sudden dry heat made the air difficult to breathe. The trees and forests looked green, but the grass and weeds looked parched. The lake spread out with barely a ripple.

She smeared insect repellent on her exposed skin and grabbed the extra water bottle from the back seat. Rock whined lightly. "Just a moment, Boy. I wouldn't forget you." She hung the bottle on a belt loop and let it bounce off her hip with a dull metallic ring as she rounded to his door.

Rock jumped out with an excitement that he always had when they hiked. Nose to the ground he followed her, while drifting from one side to the next as he sniffed. She only smelled the heavy scent of pine as they headed north into the woods.

Unleashed, Rock danced out ahead and dashed back in an excited loop. It only took a minute before she could hear Louis and then Meg ahead. The pines didn't make for a dense forest. Brush grew along the shore, or wherever the thick canopy allowed sunlight to the ground. Light weeds and native plants grew through the thick litter of brown pine needles on the forest floor. Dad would know their names. An unseen car passed on the road to her right, and the lake stretched out to her left. Despite all that she worried about, she suddenly felt calmer.

"Go ahead, Rock." Haddie gestured ahead.

He sprinted along the trail, and after just a second she heard Meg and Sam in unison. "Rock!" In as much excitement, Louis yapped.

Before she could spot them, Dad turned along the trail toward her. He wore a leather vest with no shirt and had let his beard grow out. He'd cut his hair short, and it looked darker; the shaved side of his head had almost grown out enough to match the other side. They met along the path just as she could see Sam's pink shirt and Meg's yellow dress bent over Rock's black silhouette. Insects began buzzing around as she stood.

He pulled a bent legal envelope from his vest and unfolded a single page.

Haddie could see "Lt. Tempest" written in bold letters on the back. Dad pulled out a paper, unfolded it, and handed it to her.

The handwritten letter covered the page, and by the end of the second paragraph she had no doubt that the writer had some strange delusions. There were terms that she'd want to look up and possibly feed to Terry without explaining where they came from. Maybe this tied into some conspiracy theory that would explain their context. Near the end it rang of the Unceasing philosophies; perhaps the writer wrote both or drew inspiration from the website. The ending left no doubt to the intent of the letter, "Join us, I implore you." They'd written a PO box address on the bottom. Texas. Terry had mentioned the Unceasing training in New Mexico and Texas.

Dad watched the woods behind her and up by the road. She hadn't been followed.

"Do you think this is the leader of the Unceasing?" Haddie asked.

"I've come to that belief." Dad nodded to the letter. "What do you think?"

Haddie raised her eyebrows. "Whether you should join?"

He smirked and wiped back his hair. "No. Does this person believe all this, or is it part of the ruse? Male, female? Do they truly recruit people like us, or is it an attempt to out us? What is their plan in all this?"

Sameedha and Barbara had worked for someone, or at least alluded to that. It could be the author. "Recruitment. But I can't believe that this is anything more than rhetoric and story. We were born human, we didn't come to "this world." It makes us sound like aliens. No one could believe this. It makes it hard to take any of this seriously."

"I agree, but obviously I can't ignore this." Dad's eyes flicked at the woods around them. He would have seemed paranoid if it weren't for the letter and the warrant out for his arrest.

"Can I take a picture? I want to look up some of those names. I might leak them to Terry, without explaining any of it, to see if he can find them. Maybe this person just copied it from a conspiracy."

He tilted his head and nodded. "It's a good idea, in theory. Just don't let them know about the letter. Even the Lt. Tempest will lead to questions of my age if anyone gets too much information."

"They mention immortality. That answers my question." She'd known she healed impossibly, and that it was likely. However, Aaron had used his power and seemed to age. What was the difference? Did it matter? *I'll never be able to grow old with someone.*

She gasped. "David. I told him we'd meet But I'll be in San Fran tomorrow. Damn it."

"San Francisco?" Dad asked.

"Wait." Haddie pulled out the wrong phone and went into her other pocket and pulled out her regular cell. She'd never make it back in time from San Fran. *What am I going to text? What lie?* Her heart sunk in her chest. They had no chance with all her secrets, and she could never drag him into this. Was she supposed to give up on love and relationships? *I have to try.*

She texted as truthful a message as she could, apologizing as Dad waited. "I'm really sorry but I've got to help a friend. It means going to California tomorrow. Can we make plans on Monday?" When she hit send, it hung waiting.

Haddie drooped. "No signal."

"You can send it later. What about San Francisco?" His eyes focused on her, rather than the trees.

Haddie kept her phone in hand. *David's going to hate me.* "Uhm. Terry found out there will be a fashion show tomorrow with this Lady Erica. The one attached to the Indian company that also has connections to the Unceasing. He thinks we'll be able to tell if she's the one coercing people. I'm the only one who can tell — you know — the yellow glow." Except for Aaron, but he couldn't admit it.

Dad glanced down at the ruckus that was Sam, Meg, Rock, and Louis. Frowning, he spoke quietly. "Count me in. You're driving, I assume. When do you leave?"

Haddie's eyes opened wide. "Tomorrow morning probably, we're discussing it tonight. I didn't think you'd want to go."

"This is a war, Haddie. You just read a near manifesto. I've got to keep pace with it. I can't hide from this." A tinge of anger underlaid his tone. Not at her, but at the letter most likely. He seemed to recognize his bitterness, raising his hand in apology. "When do you meet tonight?"

"You're coming to Eugene?"

"Yes. Are you meeting at the west property?" Dad leaned forward. "I'll get there early and spend the night. Why don't you leave Rock with Sam and Meg?"

Haddie just nodded, somewhat shocked and agreeing to everything he said. Intense, he'd just bulldozed into her plans. It wasn't bad; she'd hoped he might come. However, like Boise, once he seemed set to do something he went all out.

"Good, we'll talk more tonight. Sam's been missing you." He gestured.

Indeed, Sam glanced up at them from their little cluster. A trans pride patch marked the pocket of her faded jeans, and her pale skin had a light tan. She'd given Haddie time with Dad. Sam's smile grew as she watched Haddie approach, and it felt good to be back with her friend. They had talked nearly every day. Weeks felt like years. Sam skipped the last few steps that separated them and jumped to hug Haddie.

Trying to choke back the tears, Haddie whispered, "I miss you." She held Sam's slight shoulder, pressing her close. Sam clung with both hands wrapped around Haddie's back.

"I miss you, too." Sam laughed with a touch of sob thrown in. "How do you survive without me? Move out to the farm."

I don't and I can't. She had pushed away her grief over losing Sam, but now it crushed her. Haddie pulled back quickly wiping her face. "I've got a friend who needs my help — a coworker really. But I want to help him, no matter the risk or cost."

Using both hands, Sam wiped her eyes. "Of course you want to help him. That's good." She studied Haddie. "But .. .?"

"It's a risk for me, for him, and possibly friends if I'm not careful." If these Unceasing found out about Haddie, would they go after Liz and Terry? Maybe Sam being at the farm was for the best.

"Got to weigh it. Can you leave him be to go through it?"

Haddie shivered. "No."

"Then take the risk. But be careful." Brushing away a small swarm of insects, Sam added the last part quickly. She didn't know anything about Haddie's powers, but she'd seen the wounds and purpura enough to respect the danger.

Rock had taken up with Dad and Meg threw a stick for Louis, but glanced toward Haddie as she did so. *I shouldn't ignore her.*

Sam shrugged. "You can only do your best."

"And what if that best harms the person who caused this?" *Is that what I'm worried about?*

Sam kicked at the pine needles. "Pfft. Aunt Callie used to say that you reap what you sow, and it always fit to me."

Haddie gave Sam another quick hug. She always helped Haddie's doubts. "How's Meg doing?"

Jumping up on her toes, Sam shook her hair and put her hands to her back. "She loves the puppy ranch. She draws all the time. I think she's adjusting well."

Meg swiveled toward them. "Hi, Aunt Haddie." She pointed to the water. "Do you see them?"

Sam clicked and gestured for Meg to stay quiet.

Haddie turned. The deep blue water had hardly any ripples across it. She knew how far the lake stretched from driving past it to get to the east edge. There were some boats or maybe houses or docks far on the opposite end. Nothing close. "What?"

"They're like lights on the water."

Dad still crouched by Rock, but turned as well. There might have been a little mist, or a reflection from a boat's windshield that caught her eye. When Haddie finally looked back, Meg looked disappointed.

"They were closer earlier. Sam can't see them, and T had walked up to the road. You've got to sing in harmony. They know that." Meg seemed quite serious. She copied Sam's pose, putting her hands behind her back and swaying the hem of her yellow dress.

Perhaps Meg wasn't doing as well as Sam thought. "Who has to sing in harmony?" Haddie smiled politely.

"You and T." Meg seemed pleased that Haddie asked.

Haddie raised her eyebrows. "And they said that?"

Meg shook auburn locks. "No. They know it. And sometimes I can know what they know when they get close."

Dad stood up. "Okay, Meg. Let's take a little walk."

A frown settled on Meg's face. "You still don't believe me."

He shook his head. "Not believing and not understanding are two different things. Let's walk. Louis seems to be staying close, so let him off his leash for a bit."

Dad led the way, and Sam shrugged and bumped her shoulder against Haddie before following him. Rock kept pace with Dad, which brought Louis to his heels. Haddie took up the rear and glanced back and over the water. A reflection, nothing more.

Well worn, the path wove a fairly even line following the edge of the lake. The scent of pine, water, and a bit of decay near the shore surrounded them. The heat hadn't gotten that bad yet. The water and shade kept them a bit cooler. If only there were a breeze.

Dad is coming to San Francisco. The more it settled in, the more she liked the idea. It should avoid any of the rest of them coming up with some quick idea. In Boise, she couldn't help herself with Kiana captured. This time, everyone else would be safe somewhere while she scouted the fashion show.

She'd warn Kiana before Dad showed up at the house. He'd said early.

.

Haddie's burner dinged within a minute after getting back on route 58. "Read text," she said aloud. She had Bluetoothed the burner into her car. Her regular cell rarely got any use.

The text she'd written to David would be sending too. Her heart fluttered, and her stomach felt queasy. The RAV4 hadn't cooled down in the time she left the parking lot, and sweat clung along her sides and stomach.

"I found out some cool stuff about Lady Erica. She's got like no past. I'm still at the library. I'm going to be late tonight."

I really should find out about this Erica. Dad's megalomaniac fan still hung in her mind. She'd left Rock with Sam, as Dad suggested, and that felt wrong. How had he been in relationships, knowing that they would grow old without him? *Focus, Haddie.*

"Call Terry," she told the car.

"Hey, Buckaroo. Driving?"

"Yeah, what did you find out about Lady Erica?"

"Okay. She's non-existent until about twelve years ago,

then she pops up in New York. Now here's the weird stuff. She's an assistant, as Erica Landon — for six years under a fashion designer named Roberto Gabbana. Then pop, two years ago she ends up owning his company, gets this big influx of money, and takes the fashion show international. This Roberto works for her now." In the background, Terry took a breath and the keyboard of his computer clacked. "I'm trying to follow that original money, but it's buried in corporations out of Argentina."

Someone who could coerce would easily be able to take over a company. It made sense. This had to be the person who did it to Josh. So did she need to go to San Fran now? *I still want to.* Just to see her. What was their plan? They could discuss it tonight. "You're going to be late tonight? Dad's going."

"T? I haven't seen him for a year. Yeah, Livia's running late at the food bank. I'll leave the library in about an hour." He paused as something chimed in the background. The computer room at the library could get noisy. Terry swore. "Alarm's going off at my house."

Haddie glanced at the display showing the call. "What?"

"I'm pulling up the cameras." She could hear the chime in the background and the furious rattle of his keyboard. He swore again. "FBI."

"What?" Her heart skipped a beat and her eyes flicked from the windshield to her dash. She'd decelerated and reacted, pressing down on the gas. Why were the FBI at his house? *Is this my fault?* Had they raided the hillside house too? Kiana and Aaron? Surely not Liz. It had to be something to do with Terry's searches. Or the trace. If the FBI were Josh's hackers, had they figured out Terry tried to trace them? *This is all my fault.*

"Okay," Terry said. His typing slowed a little. "As long as they don't pull it from the battery backup, we're good. Glad I didn't move in with Livia, she'd freak."

Haddie winced; she'd wound her hair too tight, and it pulled against the back of her neck. "What are you talking about?"

"Sorry, sorry. I had to remote in and run a program to rewrite my local drives. And you bust my chops about conspiracies — see? I keep most stuff hidden on clouds and I'm deleting those now. They're focused on clearing the rooms and my gaming computer. One of them will eventually find the switch and trace it back to the rack in the closet. Too late for them."

"Terry. The FBI." She enunciated each letter while glaring at the dash. "They're after you."

"Yaass, pretty cool. But yeah, there's that." His tone subdued. He still typed in the background. "I'm posting about it now. I suppose I dug too deep on Lady Erica. Should I turn myself in, or do you think they'll just twist me into something like your friend Josh?" He tried to sound nonchalant, but she could hear fear in his voice now.

Will they be waiting for me at the apartment? "I'll call Andrea. See what she says."

Terry didn't reply, but she could hear his typing.

Haddie leaned across to grab her regular cell. Her hands shook as she scrambled for it. The RAV4's tires crossed the center lines of the highway, but she steered back into her lane. Was it just his digging on Lady Erica? Or did this tie into Josh? Had the FBI managed to watch them all this time? *Someone should check in with Kiana.* With one hand on the steering wheel, she tried to navigate her phone and watch the road at the same time.

"Uh, Haddie?"

"Yeah?" She brought up Andrea's contact, pausing as a semi passed.

"You might want to have your boss meet me at the FBI headquarters."

Haddie blinked. "What? Why?"

CHAPTER 16

HADDIE GLARED AT THE DASH, waiting for Terry to respond. The AC blowing out of the RAV4's vents chilled her shoulders and caused her to shiver.

What did Terry see? Had they gotten to his hard drive before he could wipe it? What was on it anyway? The FBI's raid might mean that she wouldn't be going to San Fran tomorrow. Kiana would freak over the FBI. *Aaron might just run.*

He spoke quietly, near to a whisper. "Okay. I'm burning this phone before they find me. The FBI just walked up to the front of the library." Terry had stopped typing and it sounded like he walked across the room as the background noise shifted. "I saw them through the window. Most of my data is toast by now. This search into Lady Erica has to be the reason. You've got to get to San Fran. Learn what you can. First though, call your boss, Buckaroo." His connection ended.

Haddie glanced from the dash to her console where the burner charged. *Damn.* She checked the mirror before slowing and pulling off the road. Andrea, Kiana, and then

Dad, though he might not get the message for a while. He planned on lunch at the lodge with Sam and Meg. Was this the regular FBI or the cabal that hounded Kiana?

She dialed Andrea with blood pounding in her ears. *Saturday — midday — she might be home.*

It took four rings before Andrea answered. "Hi, Haddie. What's up?" She sounded sad, or tired.

Haddie drew in a deep breath. "The FBI just arrested a friend of mine, Terry, Terrence Lipton. I don't know why. Can you represent him?"

A cat called out in the background, and it took Andrea a moment to respond. "Initially at least. Is he downtown at their office there, or in the field office in Portland?"

"I don't know, honestly."

"Okay, I'll find out." Andrea's muted tone ended in a sigh. "I'm getting dressed now. I'll call and then head down to their office on 7th."

Haddie almost asked Andrea if something else was wrong. She couldn't get distracted, though. Terry needed her help. *What have I gotten him into?* They'd raided his apartment and knew enough to hunt him down at the library. How long had they been watching him? Long enough. *I need to mention the raid.* "They probably broke into his apartment as well. The alarm is going off."

"Okay. Should we talk before I head to their office?" Andrea's tone cooled, sounding more normal.

Haddie wasn't about to mention the burner, but there'd be no record of a regular call. "I'm not in Eugene. I was driving when one of our friends told me about it. That's about all I know. Thank you, Andrea."

"I'll call you when I know something." Andrea hung up.

Haddie leaned back into her seat and groaned. She needed to get to Eugene and find out what Andrea could do. Her stomach turned, and she felt shaky. There had been too many hits all at once between Josh, Dad's letter, and now Terry. What if the FBI had raided the hill house at the same time?

She took a deep breath. "Call Kiana." As the phone rang over the speaker, she glanced at the side mirror but didn't move to get back on the highway. She needed a moment to calm herself.

"Hey," Kiana answered. "How's your father?"

Haddie raised her eyebrows. She couldn't remember mentioning the visit. "How —?"

"Sorry. He mentioned it last night. I called him after you left."

Dad told Kiana that they were meeting? *Focus, Haddie.* "The FBI arrested Terry; well, they raided his apartment and were coming after him at the college."

Kiana took a moment to respond. "That's not good."

It's horrible. Haddie closed her eyes. "He trashed his data and burner phone. How long do you think they were watching him?" *Am I worried about us, or Terry?*

"Not long, or he wouldn't have had time to burn his data. Did they go after his computers or just him?" Kiana paused just as it seemed she was about to say more.

"Computer. He had cameras and got the alarm while I was talking to him. Then they showed up at the library and he got rid of his burner phone."

"Speaking of." Kiana sighed. "We should go dark for a while. Pull our batteries until we get a better grip on what the FBI knows, or if they got his phone."

Haddie pulled her hair away from her sweaty neck and twisted it. "Okay. I'll tell Dad. He plans on getting to the house early." He might decide to cancel the whole thing, with the FBI involved. At least they hadn't raided the hill house, so maybe they were only focused on Terry's internet activity. "Unless Dad cancels now."

Kiana's tone brightened. "Thomas is coming? To the fashion show?"

"He plans to, but who knows with the FBI and all."

"I'll call him, then unplug. You should take the battery out of your burner when we hang up. I'll let Aaron know."

"Think he'll run?"

"Maybe, he's been moping in his room most of the morning." Kiana paused, sounding like she paced the floor. "Can you find out about Terry?"

Haddie let go of her hair and checked the side mirror. She needed to get back to Eugene and check in with Andrea. "That's where I'm headed now." What if Andrea couldn't get Terry out? What if they coerced him? If they were right about Lady Erica being the coercer, then she couldn't get to him while she stayed in California. Unless they brought Terry to her. *I need to get back to Eugene.* First, the battery out of the burner. "I've got to go. Be careful"

"You, too. Be careful coming to the house tonight." Kiana hung up.

Haddie popped the battery out of the burner and stared at it. *I'm really not made for this spy stuff.* She had to get back to Eugene and check in with Andrea.

Her own cell connected to the RAV4 again, and she pulled onto route 58 for Eugene.

CHAPTER 17

HADDIE DROVE the RAV4 down 6th toward downtown Eugene where the traffic thickened and slowed. The AC didn't seem able to fight off the early afternoon heat, and she needed a shower or at least a change of clothes. Both her water bottles rattled empty on the passenger seat.

She couldn't guess what Terry was going through with the FBI. *What's going on with Andrea?* Haddie had to resist calling. She'd called Liz instead during some of the ride and let her know about Terry. Every word they said she imagined someone listening to them. Now, as she neared Pearl Street, she had no plan except to park across from the Feds' building and wait. *How long?*

Wilted maples surrounded a lot with only a couple dozen cars parked in it. She'd never parked there before. Andrea's E-Class Mercedes-Benz was parked facing Pearl Street, and Haddie swung into the lot and pulled in beside her boss's car.

"Now what?" Haddie asked herself. Andrea could be hours or minutes. *I should just go home.* It felt like abandoning Terry, and she felt guilty already. There was a coffee shop on the other side of the courthouse down Pearl Street. Leaving her car parked beside Andrea's and across from the FBI seemed more like keeping a vigil than going home. A glass of tea and a bite to eat would be a welcome distraction. Turning the RAV4 off, she climbed out and instantly regretted not driving there.

The motionless air lay thick and hot across the parking lot. She nearly ran for the shade of the trees drooped over the sidewalk.

The two-story complex that held the FBI office looked dead. She expected it to be empty on the weekends. Someone must be at the office, or Andrea's car wouldn't be parked outside. The FBI had picked up Terry over an hour ago; if they were going to take him to this building, he'd be there by now. Haddie could call and see if Andrea wanted her to come inside as well. She wouldn't. Besides, for all she knew, the FBI were taking him to Lady Erica to be coerced. *I can't think that.*

By the time Haddie made it to the next block, she was sweating worse than she had on the hike with Dad. Her phone vibrated with a text before she reached the next intersection.

David texted. "Okay, I understand. But can we talk on the phone Monday? Texting leaves me interpreting and questioning each line. I do better if I can at least hear you say it."

He had taken over an hour to respond. Haddie hesitated, then she called him. "Hey."

"Hi," he said. "Thanks."

"I'm sorry about tomorrow. I really didn't want to cancel. I do want to sit and talk with you. I miss you." Haddie jogged to cross the intersection with the light.

"I miss you, too. I don't expect you to abandon your

friend though. I'm okay with it." He paused and there were muffled voices in the background. "Sometimes I just feel left out of parts of your life. Which is fine, but it's the secrets around them that make me uncomfortable. The vague excuses or the sudden trips. I guess I can live with it, but then I question why I have to."

Sudden trips — like to San Fran. She couldn't involve him. Every friend who knew about her powers was at risk. If they'd taken Terry to get coerced, then they'd all be on the run, even Liz. Haddie's jaw tightened. "Some things I can't talk about. There's a warrant out for my dad and I don't want you to get caught up in something that could hurt you." She winced at the comment. Not quite a lie, but it was an attempt to mislead David.

He remained heartbreakingly quiet for too long. "I won't ask then."

Haddie stopped in front of the café, unsure if he was going to continue. She wanted to hold him and promise she loved him. *We could meet now and not wait.*

Her phone beeped as Andrea called.

"David, my boss is calling. Can I —?"

"Understand. Call me Monday." David hung up.

Haddie sagged, staring through the window at the lone couple that sat inside with afternoon coffees. He seemed willing, but she might be messing it up again.

"Hi," she said to Andrea.

Andrea spoke quickly, her tone brusque and sharp. "I'm not sure what is going on, but I may end up filing a complaint on Terry's behalf anyway. There are no charges. The office didn't even have a record of warrants filed. I'd think they were giving me a run around, but the office genuinely seemed left out of the loop. The field agents were from Portland and are bringing him into the office in the next half hour. I'd like to know where they've been." She paused and footsteps echoed. "Meet me in the south lobby in half an hour."

Haddie sighed. "Coffee?"

"Black." Andrea hung up.

Where *had* the FBI been with Terry? She opened the door to the café, and rich coffee scented the cool air that swirled around her. The entire situation sounded exactly like the sketchy cabal within the FBI that was after Kiana. Hopefully, Andrea's interference had stopped any serious harm. Haddie caught the scent of pastries, and her mouth watered. The protein bar on the ride back to Eugene hadn't lasted long.

Balancing a tray of coffee and tea with her left hand, Haddie left the store biting into a delicious, cinnamon-sprinkled, cream-filled croissant. She smudged powdered sugar into her tank top when she tried to wipe away errant pastry flakes. She'd settled for their iced tea and finished it before she reached the FBI office.

Andrea wore an uncharacteristically simple, pale blue button-down blouse and dark slacks with her red hair loose around her shoulders. She paced along an empty hall beyond the guard and waved at him to let Haddie in the door.

Andrea's expression made Haddie hesitant, but her boss thanked her for the coffee and took a few sips before she started talking about Terry's situation. "They're really pissing me off. We're supposed to wait for the Agent in Charge before we can get any details. This is highly irregular." She motioned toward an interior door with one finger from the hand holding her coffee. "I had to prove the police's response to the alarm before they would even check into this. Any idea what they might be looking at Terry for?"

Haddie shook her head, trying to brush crumbs and sugar from her shirt. It might be better to play ignorant than outright lie.

Andrea took a deep breath in and out. "They have no charges or warrant, which would indicate something serious, but they were quick enough to state he's not being detained and they would be bringing him here." Pulling her phone out, she ended the conversation and began messaging someone with one hand.

Feeling dismissed, Haddie leaned against the wall and scrolled through social media. *Was something else bothering Andrea? Josh?* Her boss had seemed distracted and now near the point of anger. Andrea never let herself get out of control.

Haddie froze in the hall as a guard let in two FBI agents in jackets. The smaller one with a light complexion and sandy colored hair had a yellow glow to his face. His scowl would have put Detective Cooper to shame. Terry offered a nervous but grateful smile.

Andrea strode up to them. "Who's the Agent in Charge?"

The non-coerced agent, taller with a thin mustache, replied, "The ASAC will be available at this number." He handed her a business card. "Alternatively, you can email him."

Haddie stayed back, watching the coerced agent. He had noticed her as well, but focused on Andrea. His hands hung straight at his sides awkwardly. Seeing him reminded her of Josh. Would he still be at the office, digging through emails?

Terry shifted to the side away from the agents.

Andrea shook her head. "Terrence Lipton obviously is not being held. Under what grounds –?"

The coerced agent seemed to growl. "Call the ASAC." The two agents turned and started back out the doors.

Haddie raised her eyebrows; she'd never seen anyone ignore Andrea like that. Watching the glow of the coerced walk away, she stepped quickly to Terry. "What did they want?"

Andrea already had her phone out, and he gave her a glance.

"Well, at the end, after they got a couple calls, they said I was being questioned about a terrorist group that I was connected to. They didn't mention which one, and since they seemed to be packing me up to go, I didn't ask. They were a spooky bunch."

"Where did they take you?" Haddie asked.

"An empty office off 7th."

Andrea had the phone to her ear. "They can't. Not for a questioning."

Terry grimaced, somewhat comically. "And yet, they did."

She ignored him and frowned. A recording played on her phone, and she brusquely left her name and number, mentioning Terry as her client. Her nostrils flared and her lips pulled back when she spoke. "This doesn't happen. I need to file a complaint. Pro bono. Nothing much else we can do about it. What questions did they ask you?"

Terry took a deep breath, carefully avoiding a look at Haddie. "They asked about some people that I didn't know. Showed me some pictures. I seemed to frustrate them, then it seemed their boss called, and these two brought me here."

Andrea nodded. "I need to see what they come up with." She dug in her purse and took out a card. "Call the office Monday. Get in to see me. I should have something to work with by then. Meanwhile, write down every question they asked. Every name. Describe the pictures. Get me the address of the office where they took you, and any potential witnesses there." She started for the door.

"Thank you, Andrea," Haddie called out.

Terry nodded. "Yes, thank you. Amazing work." He grinned at Haddie, then tilted his head toward the guard. "Maybe we should go."

Haddie had parked right beside Andrea, so she slowed Terry once they were outside. "What did they ask you?"

He tilted his head and mocked an exasperated expression. "Why was I digging about Lady Erica. What else?"

"What did you say?"

"I started with the fact that I really dug painted ladies. I thought the short blond guy was going to hit me for that."

Haddie nodded. "He's coerced."

Terry swore. "I knew it. I mean I can't see it, but yeah. Anyway, I lied, told them that I was in some random group, which I am, and we had a side chat going on the idea that she and all fashion designers are reptilian aliens. They might have bought it. Asked me for some handles." He smiled. "I don't know who OneRun3029 and Mekalb91 are in real life, but they're jerks on the boards. I needed patsies."

"That's it?"

He shook his head. "Nope. Then they brought out Kiana's picture and Aaron's picture and wanted to know if I knew them. I figured they already would have put me and Doc together, but they hadn't seemed to. They hadn't even started showing me the pictures until they talked with someone over the phone. There were four of them."

Haddie raised her eyebrows. "What did you do?"

He grinned. "I was fairly sure that Special K was my middle-school art teacher and that she always did seem like a communist." He raised his hands with a shrug. "Then, after my answers weren't getting them anywhere, they started making calls and walking away to talk. I sort of thought they were going to off me for a minute or two. Finally, after a last call to their boss I'm guessing, they began packing me up to come here. They really did say that I was suspected of being a terrorist member engaged in hate speech. They seemed to think that I'd believe it." His smile dropped. "I don't think they're done with me."

Haddie chilled at the last comment. If they coerced Terry, she'd never be able to forgive herself. It would destroy everyone's life, but she could run with the others. Terry's life would be over. *I can't let that happen.*

They had to stop Lady Erica.

CHAPTER 18

THOMAS DROVE his Ford Transit along the on-ramp of I-5 and merged into the Eugene traffic. Heat waved off the asphalt. The sun had dropped into the western sky with little more than a cloud or two masking the bright blue. Approaching the city, metal utility towers replaced trees, dangling power lines webbed the horizon, and rooftops scattered around the road.

He passed the exit for Goshen and felt the twinge of loss for Biff and the garage. It would pass in time; it always did. He had visited old homes and cities in the past and the nostalgia would burn away as places changed. Some grew and became sights he didn't recognize, while others withered back into the ground. *Nothing stays the same.*

Sam and Meg had been surprised when he'd announced his trip. Mrs. Mitchell, who lived at the farm across from the kennel, had agreed to work more hours, and he had her in the office tomorrow and Monday. An intelligent woman in her late fifties, she'd been happy for the income and worked well with Sam and Meg, almost motherly. He'd assigned her a dedicated phone and kept the three other burners for the investigators who watched the kennel, Haddie, and the hillside house. Biff maintained his own people. Surprisingly, within seventy-two hours after the warrant hit, the police had pulled all surveillance off Haddie and the shop. Two weeks hadn't been enough to be confident, but it seemed they had accepted his flight. His old Shovelhead had been sold by someone matching his description in Mexico, plates and all.

He'd been prepared for just about anything, except for the letter. The drop-off should have been burned when he lost his investigators in Boise. *Sloppy*. However, he had a better understanding of his adversary because of it. He'd been reluctant to do more than keep a passive watchful stance on others with power, their coerced, and demons until the letter; now he would be moving to the offense.

Thomas took the exit leading to Franklin Boulevard and noted the one truck that followed him down the ramp. He slowed as he drove under the I-5 overpass. When the ramp turned to two lanes, the truck sped past with a plume of black exhaust, leaving him alone. The Willamette River peeked through the trees to his right.

Once he entered the busy streets of Eugene, there were three places where he pulled off Franklin to lap through parking lots and side streets to make sure he hadn't picked up a tail. By the time he got to 11th Avenue, he'd exhausted any concerns of being followed and took the long straight run to the rural areas west of Eugene.

He veered off before taking the road that led to the hillside house and found a winding drive with a rooster perched on the mailbox. Driving slowly up a rutted dirt road, he passed a single-story house with blue shutters and chickens in the yard. The van's clock read 5:22 when he parked under the fat oak beside Darren Robertson's pole barn. Thomas winced as he climbed out, dragging his backpack from between the seats, and slipped a fifty under the windshield wiper. He hadn't seen the old man, but he could be sure they'd watched him drive through their property. Darren would be out soon to check; the van would be safe and undisturbed.

Walking south through the oak and pine forest would lead directly to the back of the house that he lent to Kiana and Aaron. When Thomas had bought the property, he'd arranged the extra parking space with Darren.

The sap in the trees baked to a pungent mix of earthy oak and sharp pine. The insects and birds remained muted in the heat that hung stifling in the air. The grass and weeds crunched with a brittleness that begged for a good rain. It would come soon. The forest thinned at the back of his property; the previous owners seemed to enjoy fields more than woods.

The AC whirred at the rear of the house, and the curtains were drawn in all the windows. Thomas walked around to the old truck parked out front. Sweating slightly, he stepped to the door of the house and tapped on it. He could have gotten the second key from the barn in the back, but Kiana would be home at least. She expected him.

Aaron pushed paisley curtains aside to peek through the window and then undid the lock. "Hi." His eyes flicked cautiously across the forest as he stood aside to let Thomas in.

"Thanks." Thomas dropped his pack just inside the door and let his eyes adjust to the darkness.

The sounds of Kiana's footsteps came up the stairs. Yellow and orange beads adorned a set of braids that swung over one side of her rich brown face. Her cheeks curved into a smile. "Thomas."

He wished he could tell her about the letter. They shared common experiences. They'd both been on battlefields and survived the death and mayhem they presented. Loathsome tasks had been necessary, and they'd done them. "You look good."

"You've got a new style going on," Kiana said tilting her head as she appraised him. "I think I miss the long hair."

He rubbed his hair back. "Me too."

Kiana walked into the kitchen. "Coffee?" She had the pot ready to run from her gesture toward the button.

"Of course."

Aaron had retreated to his spot by the wall at the end of the counter, scrolling through his laptop. He flicked a glance at the two of them.

Thomas went to his pack and dug down to find two pre-paid phones. "I figure we'll need these for the trip." He placed one on the counter near the coffee maker and crossed the kitchen to hand the other to Aaron.

The man took it with a stiff face. "You still think this is a good idea after the FBI raid?"

The coffee maker began gurgling, and rich coffee scented the room.

Thomas shrugged. "Their focus was twofold. His inquiries into Lady Erica — and you two."

"How do you know?" Aaron stood up and placed the phone on the counter.

"Haddie picked up another phone. She messaged me. Terry's back home. The FBI hadn't expected Haddie's boss to show up, and they released him. I get the feeling it was a renegade operation." Thomas turned to Kiana. "I expect it was your friends, especially since they're showing your pictures."

Aaron's tone seemed tense. "And mine?"

Thomas nodded. "Seems that they've connected you and Kiana with Eugene and the digging into what they consider their business. Whoever they are, they're not stupid."

"And still, you think we should continue with California tomorrow?" Aaron asked.

"It's never so bad that something good can't come of it." Thomas glanced at Kiana who looked deep in thought.

"What good?" asked Aaron with a bitter tone.

"We know more now than before. The FBI are confirmed to be connected with the fashion shows and the demons which are sent after you. Money has connected the Unceasing with the raves and the fashion shows, even Boise. Everything has a connection, except for Harold Holmes, whom I believe they are looking for."

"Everything we suspected before. Which only makes the trip to San Francisco more dangerous — and obsolete." Aaron moved back to his laptop where he stared at the screen.

"I won't think any less of you if you don't go," Thomas said. *I mean it.* Sometimes survival meant hiding, and sometimes it meant racing at the enemy. This military man would not give up easily, that much was obvious. Terry would be at risk until they removed the threat, and that meant potential trouble for Haddie. The risk to Haddie and Meg made the path clear for himself, but he would understand someone making a rational decision not to get involved.

Kiana began pouring coffee. "Haddie's going to go, and you still want to go down and see this Lady Erica to protect your daughter?" She didn't seem to disagree with the idea; perhaps she just looked for conformation or motives.

"Haddie has her reasons, which I respect. She's loyal to

her friends." Thomas took the cup and sipped strong, rich coffee. Kiana made a good cup. "I have my own motives on top of protecting her."

The letter exposed the kind of man Thomas had to deal with. This would be a military campaign. *War.* If this woman was part of the army this man built — if she could coerce people — then Thomas intended to eliminate her.

CHAPTER 19

"LADY ERICA?"

She walked ahead of the older man, fully conscious of how low the back of her black dress draped. "You won't be disappointed, Eric."

The over-sixty billionaire had been coaxed by the allure of Erica and her models to invest a small pittance into her show. The General had picked an easy mark. *And I'm his prop, bait, and weapon.* They had used one of the many she had turned to shill and gain Eric's confidence, and he followed her from the investor's private dinner at the hotel to his own doom. She had as little choice in the General's game as her victim.

The suite she escorted him into would be his during his initial assimilation; it often took a few days for them to recover from her effects. The long marble room led to a windowed wall that looked over the lights of San Francisco. Night had not completely fallen, so the view had less of an effect than it could. Still, it would not compare with New York.

She led him to a couch and stepped behind the

mahogany coffee table, as though she meant to sit. As expected, he followed her as she turned. Enticing, she gestured him closer with black gloves that covered the scars left by her suicide attempts. The scars — at least those on the outside — had healed long ago.

His eyes lit bright with anticipation behind his thin glasses. *Poor fool.*

"Sit," she sang. The air rang around her, and the pain grated across her skin like embedded needles. Her knees wobbled at the fire in her joints.

Eric's eyes widened as he fell toward the couch. Visions washed away his descent and the elegant suite.

In a rocky pass of red striped stone, she faced a throng of thick, tall men in woolen robes. The air cut her lungs with the cold. She recognized the man singing behind them, sun-bright palms blazing over them. Her own throat rumbled with an overtone that protected her from his power, and she sang to the men, "Protect." Three turned and the battle among their own began.

The world spun into darkness. The deck below her pitched under her side. Wind whistled outside, and water lapped against a hull. The man who crept into her cabin had the yellow filaments of her turning winding through his face. He'd been stabbed bloody across his chest and stumbled on the attacker she'd killed. "Master?" His name was Bjon.

His attacker followed, dressed in black, bursting into the door. The last of the boarding party. "Mine," she sang.

Her last vision brought her to a rocky shore where her teenage son walked beside her under stiff winds that stank of the sea. Her hand rested on the blond boy's shoulder. It was a man's hand with hair and thick knuckles that were wound with leather and metal studs. She could not let him grow into his own power and threaten to depose her some-day. "You are mine," she sang.

The suite came back into focus as she swayed over the couch. Wincing, she dropped to the cushions beside Eric. "Tyrone." Her throat dry, her voice cracked as she called out.

Eric stared aimlessly into the room. She would assign him attendants to help him through the initial shock. Older men took the longest. If she gave him a command, he would obey, but not efficiently. Better if he rested.

Tyrone came quickly from the hall around the corner from the sitting room, concern on his face and a brandy glass and tablet already in hand.

She took the glass with trembling fingers that burned as she grasped. Shoving the pain aside, she drank a long draught of cognac. Warmth spread throughout her body, but it would do little to remove the pain. Only time did that.

"Mistress?" Tyrone motioned toward the tablet. With tawny skin and compassionate dark eyes, he waited for her gesture.

The message opened at his touch. "You have a new assignment when you are done in San Francisco. Terrence Lipton of Eugene Oregon."

So soon? She nodded dully to Tyrone. Her flesh felt seared. She finished her glass and handed it back to Tyrone. The General might just kill her before she could do the job herself. Shivering as she remembered her visions, tears eased down her painted face. Some past incarnation or ancestor had turned their own family in greed for power. Why the General thought they should be leading this world made no sense. His own actions, hers, and the visions showed nothing but selfishness and cruelty. She wanted to vomit the brandy. *I need a bath.* She had the show tomorrow and the dinner afterward to recruit new models. Then, back to Eugene. "Help me up, Tyrone. I need a bath."

The white paint covered the horrors that her powers made of her skin. It could be washed off in water, but the horrors inside were stains that couldn't be cleansed.

CHAPTER 20

HADDIE PARKED her RAV4 in front of the hillside house and turned off her headlights. The air had cooled a few degrees with sunset; at least she wanted to believe it had. It would be cooler when they left in the middle of the night. The afternoon with Terry had frazzled her. He complained about all the data they had lost, but he did so safely in his apartment, or by now, Livia's.

Am I doing the right thing? Haddie's anger had popped up frequently toward the end of the day and forced her to question her motives. She couldn't call Sam. She'd talked with Liz about Terry before he'd been released, but she hadn't answered after that. Dad had kept her busy shopping for the trip, but paranoia had plagued her at every street corner. They would go over the final details tonight with Aaron and Kiana and be off early in the morning, so she had little time left to fret. She would sleep here tonight, the fashion show would happen tomorrow, and she still had no idea how they would stop Lady Erica or help Josh.

Leaving her luggage in the back, she grabbed the drawstring bag filled with overnight toiletries. She'd managed to clear out some of the junk from her RAV4 so that people could sit and have room for their own bags. It had taken two trips, and she'd found the matching boot to the one that had sat in her closet for a year.

She paused as her regular cell vibrated in her pocket. *Andrea? Terry?*

Haddie stared at the screen.

Grace had texted, "I thought you should know that Josh's mother died a couple weeks ago. We just found out about it last night. Andrea is crushed."

The color drained from Haddie's cheeks. *Did I cause this?* "How did she die?" she texted.

"In her sleep from her illness. It explains why Josh acted strangely. He still wants to come to work Monday, which is why I thought you should know before you got to work."

Haddie hadn't caused it, and Grace could only make the assumption about what affected Josh. She didn't know and hopefully never would. When had Lady Erica gotten to him? Before his mother died, or after?

"Sorry to bring the bad news. See you Monday."

"Thank you," Haddie texted. Her throat felt thick. If she couldn't fix this, how could she ever look at Josh again?

She'd known something had bothered Andrea. The woman had never said anything about it, and never hesitated to help Terry despite what she might be going through over her friend's death. *I didn't thank her enough.* Did Josh experience the pain of his mother's death, even coerced? When Aaron had spoken of those he had accidentally coerced, it sounded as though his unintended victims had moved on with their lives. She couldn't ask him.

Moving toward the door to the house, she frowned. *Had Dad not arrived yet?* Perhaps he'd parked elsewhere on the property. The door was locked, so she tapped, and her frown vanished when Dad opened the door to let her in. The kitchen smelled of cooked fish and garlic with a mix of spices she didn't recognize. Kiana leaned against the counter by the sink, and Aaron sat at his spot by the wall.

"How are you doing?" Dad asked.

"Not great. I'm worried for Terry, and I just found out that Josh's mother died sometime around Boise."

Kiana frowned. "Poor kid. I wonder if he knows?"

Haddie fought tears. Did he feel trapped inside his own mind? What was it like for him? "I can't think about it right now. I need to talk about what we can do rather than dwell on what's happened."

"Gumbo?" Kiana motioned toward the stove. "I can heat it up."

Haddie shook her head. She'd grabbed Chinese food with Terry. "What's the plan for the morning?" She strode toward the living room. "I need to sit."

Dad strolled into the living room but didn't sit. "I want to get there a couple hours before the show, so we've got just over five hours before I want to leave. We'll need time near the hotel to get you dressed."

"You said you'd get dressed as well."

He nodded. "I need a little time. We might not get much farther than the lobby, but the odds are better if we look like we belong. Terry had mentioned a model recruitment that they often do around these events. We'll use that to get closer."

Haddie frowned. She hardly considered herself having a model's body with her thick thighs, but she understood the ruse. "And if there is no recruiting going on? I couldn't find any mention of it."

"Then we're just there to find out how to interview for positions. It would not be unusual."

Kiana smirked as she dropped into the couch. "They will be jumping to recruit you. You don't have to worry about it."

"Let's assume we get in, close enough to see the glows around their eyes, then what?" Haddie leaned forward, twisting her hair around her hand.

Dad looked down at the floor. "I'd rather we play it by ear. However, there seem to be three general options: we could head back with a confidence that we'd found the person responsible for coercing people, we could try and persuade her to release Josh, or we could remove her."

"Remove, like kill?" Haddie's eyes widened.

He nodded. "You wouldn't have to be involved. I can infiltrate late that night if they stay at the hotel or intercept if they leave."

"What would that do to Josh?" Haddie looked directly at Aaron.

His face tightened and he turned to his laptop ignoring her. She hadn't meant to do that. Would he know?

"I would hope it would free him and anyone else she'd coerced. We can't know until we try." Dad wiped his hair back, looking up to study her reaction.

He had to know she couldn't accept that. "We can't just leave, and I'm not going to risk killing her; we have to persuade her." *If I knew it would free Josh, could I kill her in cold blood?*

He nodded in a way that reminded her of arguments they'd had in the past. "Okay. How? Torture her? Could you do that? If you could, how do we get her away from all the coerced we expect to see? Let's say we do. Do we drug her so that you can do the torture alone? We can assume that you can resist her like you did with the others. I can't. Kiana can't. So we can't be around her when she's conscious."

I don't need to torture her. If they captured her, which sounded difficult, then Lady Erica could release Josh if she wanted to go free. Eventually she would. *How do I capture her — alone?* Dad could learn to resist, but how would they practice? They had five hours and eight hours on the ride to plan. "A tranquilizer gun. You must know a vet who could get you that."

He shrugged. "In San Francisco midday tomorrow? Let's say I can. You plan on wandering into the hotel with it, or sneaking in that night? A hostile extraction needs careful planning and understanding the target's patterns. We have neither. I think our options are gather data and leave, or finish it before it gets worse."

She could sense from his tone that he preferred the latter. Haddie slumped in her chair, suddenly feeling tired. She'd be stupid if she thought she could get a gun into the fashion show and then find a time to get Lady Erica alone. Dad, at least, would need to be close to help her move the body. The woman stood taller than Haddie's 6'1". Someone would come looking for her. *I can't just give up and leave Josh like this.* "These tranquilizer guns, can they be pistols?" She'd only seen them as rifles on safari documentaries.

"Yep. I won't go there though, since the drugs can either overdose in one shot or never knock them fully unconscious. I wouldn't risk any of us in that situation without proper planning. You're not trained for infiltration, so we can't have you break into her room in the middle of the night.

"So you're just going to kill her?" Haddie flushed. Angry and disappointed, she glared at him.

"Technically, that is war. She has no concern for her

targets. They get thrown at you, us, as disposable weapons. Think of the men who died in Boise. She did that."

Haddie couldn't go with the express purpose of killing someone. "Promise me you won't, or I won't go."

He nodded. "I promise not to kill her during this trip unless we agree to it after we see the situation. I can't agree to you trying a kidnapping. Also, if I decide to act on my own, outside of this trip, then it's on me. You might have to accept Josh's fate in your decision."

"We'll decide when we get there." She hated that her Dad was so willing to kill someone, but part of her agreed with his logic. What if Lady Erica went after Terry or Liz after she'd stopped Dad? *I'd hate myself.* She didn't argue over his obvious intention to continue his plot to kill the woman. There had to be something they could do for Josh. Haddie's cheeks warmed. She hadn't had reservations about killing Lady Erica; she'd only been worried about getting her own hands dirty and the effect it might have on Josh.

Kiana leaned forward. "I'm asking you both, since I've been thinking about it. Would abilities work with a secure gag in place?"

Haddie shrugged. "I think so. It doesn't seem to matter what the sound is, it just starts it or helps me focus it."

"Gags don't stop it. I don't think sound is necessary at all, but a hum will get you there. Trust me." He frowned. Obviously, he'd had an experience that Haddie hadn't witnessed in her visions. "It's getting late. We'll have time to talk on the ride. You coming, Aaron? You should get some sleep if you are."

Aaron had turned to his laptop, scrolling through posts in some chat room. He shrugged. "Probably, but I'm not getting involved. I doubt I'm coming back here."

Kiana gave Haddie a concerned look. However, it

wasn't that surprising. Terry's incident with the FBI and Josh's state were bringing the danger closer to Eugene. Kiana should disappear as well.

"Okay." Dad nodded his head to Haddie. "I've got you set up. C'mon. Try and get some sleep."

Haddie winced as her joints protested when she got up from the chair. *I shouldn't judge Aaron so hard.* He didn't need to risk his life for her or her friends. "I hope you come tomorrow, Aaron." She passed him as he shot her a suspicious look. *I meant it.* She'd been hard on him. Her nerves had been frazzled from Josh and Terry. "Good night, Kiana. The gumbo smells great." Why couldn't she go back to a life where she didn't always worry someone was about to attack her or her friends?

"Good night, Haddie." Kiana didn't say goodnight to Dad. *Did they plan on talking later?* They seemed to be on the phone a lot, from their comments.

Haddie glanced back. Kiana moved toward the stairs down to her room. Did they have something going on? Haddie raised her eyebrows. Dad had never gotten with anyone since her mother. She'd asked about it when she was in high school, but he'd ignored her, claiming that he wasn't ready. *Are you ready now, Dad?* Kiana had no idea about him — the immortality part at least.

Haddie waited until they reached her bedroom. "Dad? You and Kiana?"

He rubbed his broken nose, but she could see a slight blush. "Maybe. Would that bother you?"

Maybe a little. "How do you do it? How do you fall in love with someone and let them fall in love with you, knowing that they'll grow old without you?"

"I've tried not to, but eventually someone comes along that you can't resist. I dye my hair a little grayer as time goes on. For me it is probably easier than it will be for you to look old. You can avoid relationships if you want, but you'd be missing a lot of what makes life worth living — being there for others." He shook his head. "Get some sleep."

Haddie let him close the door as he left, like he'd done most of her life. What did she think about him wanting to kill Lady Erica in cold blood one minute, and being in a relationship with Kiana the next?

I've got to sleep.

It would be a long day tomorrow. Terry wasn't safe. She had mentioned taking Livia camping, but he'd made a face. Josh needed the most help. In a few hours, she'd see this Lady Erica for herself. *I need to stay focused.*

CHAPTER 21

HADDIE DROVE her RAV4 in the dark with her headlights lighting the trees that sprang up along the country road heading southwest. The AC blew cool air, and the scent of coffee hung in the car. The stars had a couple hours before the sun would disturb them. They'd be on I-5 by then. Their trip would take them against the Pacific Coast Ranges and into some steep slopes. She'd done this trip with Dad a couple times and once with Derrick. Maybe, some day, she could enjoy it with David. Today, dread filled her chest as they drove.

I don't know what the right thing is. She'd awakened angry. Dreams, her subconscious, or both nagged at her. She wanted to abduct Lady Erica, tie her and Josh in opposite chairs, and force the woman to free him. Dad had been right in his concerns. However, she couldn't let him kill the woman and risk Josh.

"Heading into rain." Aaron sat directly behind her, possibly to avoid her glare; she'd snapped at him during breakfast.

Kiana leaned over to look at his phone, and Haddie

caught her eye in the rear-view mirror. Haddie had been awkward getting food ready and prepped for the trip, and Kiana had picked up on it. She kept rubbing her earlobe in a nervous tick.

Dad stared out the passenger window. "Where does the rain start?"

"Central Douglas County through northern California. I'd guess in the next hour," Aaron answered.

Kiana smiled. "Sounds like my shift at the wheel." Behind her, the black dress that Haddie picked up for the fashion show hung in the back. It seemed to squeak at her hips when she tried it on.

"Shotgun," Dad said before glancing over at Haddie with a light grin. He'd offered her similar looks throughout the morning when she'd been annoyed.

She had been acting a bit spoiled, but he remained unapologetic during their quick breakfast. *It's his life.* Haddie didn't expect him to remain celibate for a mother she barely remembered, it just came as a surprise. Dad had already moved away with Sam and Meg, so a relationship with Kiana couldn't take any more of Haddie's time. *He should be happy.*

She should have been meeting with David today, and maybe patching things up. Josh's coercion by Lady Erica had disrupted what might have been a good weekend. It's her fault, not Josh's.

When it came time to switch after two hours of driving, Haddie turned onto the exit for Wolf Creek nestled high in the hills. The first gas station they came to in the early morning had lights on and a black Ford Colorado sitting by the pumps. The air had a solid chill to it, and the stars still burned brightly. Haddie winced as she stretched and collected her tea and phone. Dad went inside to pay with cash while Kiana stood and yawned on the other side of the RAV4. *I need to stop acting like a child.*

Haddie started walking toward Kiana. "I don't see any clouds; maybe the rain passed us."

"I saw the radar on his phone. We're going to get it." Kiana paused as if to say something, then shrugged and smiled. "I've gotten used to the cooler weather, but I grew up in rain."

Get past this. "Sorry I was a grump this morning. It's not really you guys. In the middle of all this," Haddie said, motioning toward the car, "I'm trying to get back with David, and here I am off on another secret road trip."

Kiana smiled, seeming grateful. "Thanks. Did you call him? Let him know?"

Haddie chuckled. "This time, yes. I'm trying to be conscious of that. I'm not sure how he really took it, though."

Dad had come out, striding toward the pumps, and Kiana turned toward the driver's door. "His loss if he doesn't hold on for the ride."

I'm not sure of that. Haddie climbed into the back, and Aaron didn't look up. She wouldn't have been stuck with such difficult decisions if he would just try and free Josh. However, could Lady Erica just sneak back and coerce Josh again? Her burner vibrated as she slid onto the seat, and she dug the phone out of her pocket.

A Eugene number she didn't recognize showed on the screen. "Hello?" asked Haddie.

Liz answered, "Sorry I didn't answer yesterday. I slept most of the afternoon. Went out and got a new phone, obviously, but didn't have the energy to do anything but crawl into bed."

Dad clattered at the side of the car, filling it.

"Feeling better?" Haddie asked.

"Much. Do I ever get up this early? But now, I can't sleep anymore. How's Terry?"

"Warm in bed with Livia, I imagine." Haddie cocked her head as Dad finished pumping and slapped the gas flap closed.

"Aren't you worried that they'll come after him again? Maybe do the same thing to him as they did to Josh?"

Haddie nodded to herself. *That's exactly what I'm worried about.* "Yeah, I imagined something like that. We're on the road now to San Fran." Dad slid into the seat in front of her with a grunt. Kiana started the RAV4.

Liz laughed. "I'd hope so. I don't normally call this early. So, what's the plan?"

"We're just going to see if we can confirm if Lady Erica is our person. Nothing more." Haddie spoke firmly with her eyes focused on the back of her dad's head. They'd never really been at odds like this, when he intended to do something she disagreed with, though there had been plenty of times the opposite was true.

Liz's voice came through car's speakers as it grabbed Haddie's burner. She'd been talking with Kiana last night on the ride to check whether they needed any last minute supplies. "Won't that just leave Josh stuck?"

Haddie fumbled with her burner, then shrugged. "You're on speaker with Dad, Kiana, and Aaron. Sorry. We just got gas and started the car."

"Hi guys. Gals." Liz sounded happy.

Kiana answered brightly, but both Dad and Aaron barely mumbled a hello.

Liz continued. "If this Fashion Lady is the one doing the coercing, and she dies, do you think it'll be like Sameedha where everyone she affected is released?"

Dad leaned to peer back at Haddie between the seats.

"We can't know that," Haddie said, a bit too emphatically. "What if it just left him in limbo? I can't risk that with Josh."

"Hmm. Do you think she can reverse it? But how could you force her?" Liz had adopted that far off tone she got when she started mulling over a problem. "These coerced must have some sense of internal impulse. She can't be telling them all to eat, sleep, and run to the bathroom. More than likely, she gives them overarching goals, or direct commands, and that becomes their guiding purpose, but they have to retain some self-control over their body functions. I'd try it."

Haddie raised her eyebrows. "So kill her? That's your suggestion?"

Liz sounded flustered. "I guess. I mean, I shouldn't say that, but from a purely clinical rationale it would make sense."

Leaning her head back, Haddie stared at the headliner. *Am I the only one who can't accept this?* She couldn't just go around assassinating people, even if they threatened her friends. She'd already killed more coerced than she could accept and a roomful of innocent ravers. It plagued her some nights. *How would I accept it if they got to Terry?* She *could* just let Dad loose; he obviously intended to kill Lady Erica anyway. *Could I live with being a part of that?*

I can't. Haddie lowered her head and stared through the seat in front of her. "We're not going to San Fran to kill her."

Rain pounded welcoming silence on everyone in the car, and Aaron closed his eyes. The scent of petrichor had come with the onslaught of rain and lingered in the car. The headlights had barely cut the rain with dim gray beams. Haddie only seemed to glare. She had been in a foul mood all morning.

Aaron did not intend stay too close and had booked a room away from the hotel. Kiana might jump into the fray, but he intended to get whatever information he could and move south near the border of Mexico. If it looked dangerous, he would leave without learning anything more.

Haddie's alternating moods were warranted. She wanted to help her friends, but he was not willing to risk using his power, and she was unwilling to accept that. Boise had been terrifying. For the weeks since, his nightmares had returned, incorporating the visions from college that came after he first used the power. He had hoped to leave those behind.

He did not blame Haddie; she did not understand the

terror that gripped him. She and Thomas could use their powers all they liked. *They can think me a coward.*

For the sake of everyone, it would be better for her to let Thomas kill Lady Erica than hold out for some hope that Josh's condition could be reversed. She wanted an easy path, but this trip would likely end up like Boise. They would get too close. These Unceasing were better organized than anyone expected. Perhaps Thomas had some measure of their capabilities.

In Boise, Barbara Stevens had quickly identified the investigators who worked for Thomas. It could be, as he suggested, that he felt pressured into moving quicker than he had planned. Kiana was the only one qualified to consider setting up an operation, since she at least had been trained; however, she rarely took the initiative. Haddie and Thomas tended to be the driving force in their group. *I have no interest in leading anyone.* The Unceasing had an organization and hierarchy, which was what he needed to be searching for to find all the connections and track them to a source. *I'm betting New York.*

The road curved, and Aaron looked into the shifting gray. Pines caught the headlights as they swayed with the wind.

Haddie slouched with her knees folded high up the back of the passenger seat with her eyes closed, as if she might be trying to sleep. Her fingers twitched about her phone. Did she worry about Terry? Aaron could respect her loyalty, but she did not see how she drew everyone into her situations. Perhaps she recognized it and plowed forward anyway. If Aaron stayed in Eugene, he would be drawn in one time too many and end up using his power in self-defense. *It would destroy me.*

His best option would be to get out while he could.

Traveling to California would get him started south, and close to the border of Mexico seemed a viable destination.

When he had first seen Haddie in action on the ski lift, he had been terrified that she worked for whomever had created the demons. When he had time to accept and study her powers, it had altered his hypothesis and included his own unexplained behaviors. The genetic continuation between Thomas and Haddie shifted his paradigm once more. In all, Terry's connection to Haddie had been suspect at first, but later a benefit as she had multiple direct interactions with the demons. Aaron's first assessment had been that a closer relationship with Haddie would give him the potential to research the powers, but it had turned dangerous too quickly. *I could be drawn in and use my powers.* That could not happen.

His departure would have to come quickly. They would not be surprised.

Haddie obviously considered him useless and a coward, which he was, in this circumstance. She would drag them into disaster and Kiana might not make it out alive. *I will.*

CHAPTER 23

THOMAS RODE in the passenger seat as Haddie navigated the midmorning San Francisco traffic. The rain had eased off a few hours before they'd stopped for breakfast, and the sun shone in a brilliant blue sky while light fog played along the edges of the road and flowed across water. The heat had stopped blowing from the vents, and the SUV smelled slightly musty from tightly packed people and coffee. Horns and rushing cars sounded around them.

Starting far outside of what he considered San Francisco, the metropolis seemed to pack houses into every available nook and left only some of the rougher hilltops and the water to nature. *It's spread.* The city had changed in the past eighty years since he'd come down to pick up three vintage Harleys and a Norton. It had been just before World War II, and the California cities were deep in the effects of the economic times. Poverty had seemed to draw even more people to the cities, packing them into dark streets. He'd seen similar in Europe, where people starved in streets while fish, game, and fields waited beyond the borders. Today, they passed tightly packed residences and flourishing businesses that promised affluence, though he could be sure poverty still survived in the forgotten crevices of the metropolis. As they crossed over the water, he saw a juxtaposition of mechanical monuments to man's industrious nature and a wide swath of water that faded into misty hills and islands that made up the bay. Barges and square shapes in the fog ahead hinted at the city they approached.

He'd booked a room at the hotel that hosted the fashion show in case security was tighter than he expected, and two rooms in another across the street where they would be staying. His investigator, Crow, had connections with a woman who knew San Francisco, and she had scouted the area the night before. So far, the images she sent were little more than he could have gotten online. *This is too rushed.*

Hopefully he could restrain Haddie. She'd have come to San Francisco without him. If she tried a foolish extraction, he'd eliminate the threat and get her out. Otherwise, he'd contacted a tracing specialist who might get him closer to whoever wrote the letter. Lady Erica had to work for him. She seemed to be serving as a lieutenant, recruiting troops for his movement. The organization's positions and structure made more sense when he regarded it as a military command. The raves had been funding the war effort. Barbara in Boise had been logistics, perhaps moving weapons including the coerced soldiers and demons, lieutenants like Lady Erica. There may have been an internal hierarchy, including those who sought Harold Holmes. *And my descendants.* His actions in Vietnam had brought down the disaster within his last family and orphaned Meg. He needed to find the leader and put a stop to this, before any more of his family died.

"It's beautiful," Kiana said from behind him.

He glanced at both sides and settled on the hazy hills of dark green. "It is." In the parts of the upper northwest and into Canada, he could find similar spectacular views. *Here, the fog hides the wounds left by man.* He didn't mention more, but hoped someday he could take her there. Last night had been a tender reminder of what he'd been missing since Haddie's mother had been killed. He and Kiana hadn't rushed into passion — partly because of the crowded house, but more because he wanted to savor the contact of holding someone.

"I would have thought we could see the Golden Gate bridge from here." Haddie glanced at him as she spoke, and then leaned as if searching.

Both bridges had been new when he had last visited. "Keep your eyes on the road. I'll let you know when it appears."

"I'm not going to get in an accident." She frowned and pulled her hair from behind her neck. *Too white.* Even though gray and white had become a style as of late, it still made her stand out.

"What color wig did you bring?" he asked.

"Blonde. I thought it looked more like a model." She twisted her hair and tilted her head. "You're going to keep your word, even after Liz's comment?"

"Not to kill the woman while we're here?" he asked.

Haddie nodded.

"Even though Sameedha's effects disengaged after you interrupted her? Yes." He resisted smiling. "As you'll keep yours not to attempt an abduction or try to force her to release Josh. It's too dangerous."

"When will you be killing her?" Aaron spoke up from the back. He had said little during the trip, and now he wanted to start conflict.

"I've revised that assessment, Aaron. I want to find out who she reports to." Thomas didn't look back, focusing instead out the window toward the bay. The question had been meant to incite. *I don't appreciate that.*

Haddie turned toward him. "Really? How?"

"I've contacted someone who specializes in tracing and intercepting messages. No guarantees, but it might be worth the time and money, if we can get a link up the chain." He'd been looking for something similar with those who tracked Meg. The initial investigators had been setting up the framework in Boise before he'd mistakenly moved up the timing.

Haddie seemed pleased at the answer. Eventually her emotions would return and the sense of urgency to save her coworker, but for now she didn't have to be concerned with Lady Erica's death. Perhaps that would help her maintain restraint.

His phone rang with a number he didn't recognize. He'd memorized everyone's and tried to get Haddie to do the same. He motioned her silent. "Hello?"

An automated message started. "We've been trying –" He hung up with a growl, and Haddie laughed.

"The spammers already have your number." She wore a happy smirk.

Good to see her smile. He'd been agitated by the letter the previous night when they'd talked. Kiana's presence helped him think clearly, and she'd agreed with his new plan. *I just have to keep Haddie safe today.* His people could take the risks from here. He would have aborted the trip if he thought Haddie would. Instead, he would keep it a simple confirmation and get her out of San Francisco safely.

"There's your Golden Gate bridge." He pointed ahead to his right.

PART 4

These people squander their lives meaninglessly, while we could be their unceasing and devoted guides.

CHAPTER 24

Down a dank hallway, Haddie dragged a suitcase behind her with the black dress hanging over her shoulder and her purse clutched in her hand. The hotel that Dad had booked sported a clean lobby, but the ride up a slow elevator smelling like sweat had made her question his choice. The walls had a faded red and gold design and had scuff marks along them. The gray carpet had suspicious stains, and she subconsciously held her breath at points. The lone window at the end of the hall had flimsy curtains, and she could see through to the gray wall of the building beside the hotel. She'd expected something nicer, for no particular reason except for Dad's usual selections. He seemed to avoid the seedier places; however, this one was across the street from the fashion show.

Dad nodded toward a room. "That's you, ladies. Ready in half an hour so we can slip in before it gets too busy, okay?"

Haddie nodded as Kiana unlocked the door with a beep.

He slapped Aaron on the shoulder. "You and me, Aaron."

Aaron cringed as Dad's hand remained on his shoulder, walking him to the adjacent room. Their door beeped at their keycard as Haddie lugged her suitcase through a door that tried to close too quickly.

Kiana tossed her small duffle on the first of two beds and looked about the sparse room decorated with a familiar landscape over the nightstand between the beds, a TV sitting atop a bureau on the opposite wall, and heavy curtains covering a window at the end of the room. "Almost lunchtime, but I'm not thinking room service is an option."

Haddie wedged open the closet door and hung her dress there. It didn't look too wrinkled. The AC kicked on and rattled under the window. Lukewarm air that reminded her of a wet dog blew at her as she put her suitcase on the bed and opened it. She stared at the contents, twisting her neck to release some of the tension.

Kiana found a Chinese menu in the drawer of the nightstand and waved it in the air. "Room service."

"I saw restaurants on the way in." Haddie pulled out toiletries and her strapless bra.

Motioning in a circle around her face, Kiana said, "Facial recognition." She had a wholesome smile and today she beamed. Whatever she and Dad had been up to last night suited her well. Haddie could remember the somber Special Agent she'd first met. Kiana had been intimidating, especially because Haddie had recently killed Dmitry and expected someone like the FBI to arrest her.

Haddie pulled out the heels she planned to wear and grimaced. She'd never done well dressing up for weddings and the like, and this seemed out of her league completely. *I'm going to stand out.*

"Nice shoes." Kiana dropped onto her bed wearing an easy smile.

Haddie placed the shoes on the bed. "I guess. I don't do great in heels."

"You'll do fine. It's not like you're going dancing."

"Running more likely." The room felt too hot. "I don't want this to be like Boise, but I'm not sure what we plan on doing will be any help. I am obviously not a model."

"You could easily be a model, you've got the legs for it." Kiana shrugged. "There shouldn't be any trouble, and it will help to confirm that we're focused on the right person. If there aren't many coerced attending, or none, then we need to revise our assumption. Most of my work in the FBI was confirming bad leads or assumptions so we could close in on the truth."

What will I do if it's not Lady Erica? They had too much proof it was. The woman hadn't gotten to her position in the company and been funded like she was for no reason. They had to be using her to coerce. It wouldn't make sense otherwise. It still didn't fix Josh. *Doesn't get Dad any closer to whoever wrote the letter.*

She shook out the blonde wig and stared at it. *Why did I pick blonde?*

Kiana leaned back in the bed and grabbed the remote. "You better get going. Thomas is going to be waiting in that hall."

Haddie drew in a breath and collected her bra, wig, make-up, and toiletries. "Yeah. He's probably there now."

She almost felt like bailing on the idea. *I won't.* Her stomach turned queasily. Taking a deep breath, she retrieved her black dress and headed into the bathroom.

After fifteen minutes, she stared at the mirror and shook blonde hair across bare shoulders. Her eyebrows stood out too much, and there was far too much cleavage. She grimaced and made the image worse. It would have to do. She grabbed her spent piles and hurried into the room.

Kiana had the news on; some man was discussing weather patterns and promising that the rain would hold back until Monday. It seemed that the weather they'd driven through moved south.

Whistling, Kiana said, "That's right." She smiled. "You've got this."

Haddie's cheeks warmed. "Thanks." She did appreciate the encouragement. She piled her clothes on the bed and sat to put on her shoes, feeling the dress tug in uncomfortable places. It held tight on her hips, and barely left any room for her thighs to move. Finally, purse in hand, she headed for the door.

Kiana's tone held a serious note. "Be careful. Stay sharp. My shoes are staying on, in case you need me."

Haddie swore and dug her phone out of her pants. She showed it to Kiana. "Thanks for reminding me." *I need to focus.* All she had to do was take a good look around. They weren't going to be kidnapping anybody in the middle of the fashion show. *Certainly not in this dress.* The more she thought about it, the less chance she had of getting Lady Erica to free Josh. They'd have to do something eventually, but what?

Dressed in a black suit, Dad waited outside in the dank hall. He gave a nod of approval and handed her an ID.

"Hilda?" Haddie asked. She'd been photoshopped with light brown hair. When had Dad done this?

"You left your ID hidden in the car?" He straightened a dark blue tie. He looked good, and older.

"Just like you told me to." Haddie opened her purse and slid the ID inside. She let out a breath. *Hilda.*

He held out an arm to escort her. "My name's TJ."

She laid her hand on top of his wrist as they headed for the elevator. The scenario reminded her of being a kid and playacting with him. He'd been great at make-believe. "What does TJ stand for?"

"TJ." He didn't smile.

The elevator door opened. *I'm doing this.* Haddie stepped inside.

CHAPTER 25

"Lady Erica?"

She stood at the opening of the curtains, looking at the rows of seats set up around her runway. Carolyn had walked up beside her with clipboard in hand and waited for her response.

The air had an electrical tinge to it, perhaps from the lighting. *I need to have Andrew double-check it.* Two of Dylan's monstrosities stood by the main door in their human shells with glowing orange eyes, barely controlled by bone pendants that she'd bonded them to. Wrapped in black suits and ties, she had a vague memory of each from the bonding she'd placed on them in New Mexico. That had been months ago. Dylan hadn't needed her lately, and she hadn't asked why. Dylan worked closely with the General, and she only became involved when they needed to be bonded to someone other than Dylan.

In this case, me. "Yes, Carolyn? What is it?"

"Ken's second outfit is missing the belt. We've checked the bus twice." Carolyn had added blonde highlights along light brown hair. It made her look mottled. In her late thirties now, she had been one of the first bondings. Erica's markings glowed in and out through Carolyn's glasses.

"The jacket pocket."

"We've checked."

"Send the new girl back to the ranch. There might be time. Otherwise — I'll think of something when the time comes."

Erica dismissed Carolyn with a wave and continued watching her new guards. *Why had the General thought I would need extra security?* She had her own. Too little had been explained about her acolyte Sameedha. Erica had experienced a sense of camaraderie with her over the years. She had worked with the others and would be called on again to work with Dylan when he needed to bond his freaks to someone else. But with Barbara and Araki mysteriously gone, who would she attach the monsters to?

This past year had become more hectic as the months progressed. Sudden deviations, such as this new man in Eugene, became commonplace. The General assured her that his plans had advanced and that the world would crumble before them and arise at their feet. She neither wanted the world to be underfoot nor destroyed. *I don't have the luxury of options.*

The creatures didn't move. Their orange eyes watched her like predators. The trips to the horse farm in New Mexico had been horrifying. Dylan had a cavern filled with them where these two had been selected. The General knew her distaste of them and had not sent them to her until now. Sameedha had loved the freaks and worked with Dylan to create specialized animals — pets she'd called them. *Sickening. Are these two going to stay with me after tonight?*

Araki had made her feel safe when Erica first started

binding them. The initial attempts had been horrifying, and only the General had been able to restrain Dylan's rage when the creatures had been destroyed in their efforts. Later it had become a simple enough procedure with little risk. Araki had moved on to work with Barbara.

Taking a deep breath, she closed the curtain, though the eyes remained. She had a show to run, no matter what threat the General perceived. These shows had been her passion, before and after she learned of her powers. She'd been allowed to maintain the fashion shows as an easy front to her travels and to gain access to the General's potential targets. Despite the threat that the new security implied, she would enjoy today as well as she could, and even the party this evening might prove interesting. She wouldn't have to worry about tomorrow yet.

The models clustered in the back getting their first outfits in place. Young women and men, only a few of them under her bindings, wore the new summer line. More waited in the service hall behind the room. Carolyn had disappeared as had Andrew, but Tyrone waited a few steps behind her. She gestured to him. "Let's find Andrew."

CHAPTER 26

HADDIE'S SHOES made too much noise on the marble floor and their sound seemed to echo, despite the clamor of people's voices. Scents ranged from perfumes to the flowers that filled heavy vases. The ceilings had delicate golden designs that helped her determine the actual shapes of the rooms amid the clutter of decoration and guests who milled about. Tall cream and brown marble pillars stood as high as two or three stories. The lavish detail gave a sense of the European castles she'd seen during an art class; they had made her want to visit Europe. She felt hidden and obscure. The signs that announced Lady Erica's fashion show were unhelpful, but Dad seemed to be moving in a concise direction. If he didn't know where they headed, he acted like it.

The variety of people ranged in every way, except for the sense of affluence they exuded. The level to which some dressed she would have imagined as royalty, which seemed to fit in the grand hotel. *I don't belong.* There had been no sign of any coerced; however, the opulent setting distracted her each time she tried to focus.

Awe gave way to a tense breath as she spotted her first coerced. "Dad," she whispered.

He took a moment, and then responded, "Well, that's our first sign."

They had turned into a large foyer where a group of three couples sat in a cluster of chairs and couches in the center. Past them, the coerced man waited beside double doors leading into a hall. Another foyer lay to their right through an archway. Haddie looked at the walls to each side of the coerced, but no glowing shapes were there. She imagined the event lay down that corridor.

"Down there?" she asked.

Dad walked them slowly to the right, getting a better view into the room beyond the arch. Three hotel staff in uniform were setting up a table with blue skirts and a pair of chairs. He paused and looked back at the double doors. "I think so. Do you see anything other than that one?"

"No."

A loud man wearing a brown suit and a white turtleneck entered the foyer and called out to someone who was sitting in the middle among the group. A heavier, bearded man in a shiny blue suit followed, carrying a letter-sized folio. They didn't join the people at the couches, but headed directly for the double doors, exchanging greetings as they ambled past. When they reached the corridor, the bearded man produced two cards and handed them to the coerced. They were waved down the hall.

"We're not getting down that hall without invitations," Dad said. He rubbed his hair back and glanced at her.

He's not going to mug someone, is he? The plan had been simple: get close to the fashion show, if not inside, and gauge the number of coerce involved. The one glowing face only indicated that Lady Erica's fashion shows were tied to the same organization as Samheedha and Barbara. Haddie had expected to get turned away at the doorway to the room, where she would have been able to scan for glowing faces, not down the hall. They could wander about this maze of a hotel for a bit longer, or perhaps wait for the show to finish and the crew to exit. Would they leave out the front lobby? There had to be other exits. "What are you thinking?"

He led her into the adjacent room where the hotel staff worked. "First, we continue through these halls surrounding the ballrooms. We might get along an exterior wall close enough for us to see something. If that doesn't work, then I'd look for an unlocked service entrance, maybe in an empty ballroom, and see if I can get close down the back halls."

Neither sounded like a sure plan to get close to Lady Erica. "It sounds like you're leaving me out of it."

He looked down at her outfit. "You'd stand out in a service hall."

In the smaller foyer, there were two doors and a short corridor to another, but with three hotel workers setting up, it seemed bad form to try the doors. The staff watched them as they worked, and Dad brought her to a vase of lilies to smell. "We'll head back out and turn left where we went straight."

"I have no idea where you're talking about."

"Pay attention as we walk. You need to keep a map going inside your head."

Not likely. She could keep roads straight, but big buildings like this and college took repeated trips before remembering the layout. It hadn't occurred to her that she'd need to figure out a maze.

Dad walked them toward the archway when a door opened near a table that the staff were setting up. A worker, a young man dressed in a uniform different from the hotel, kicked out the stop to prop the door open. Haddie tugged lightly, but Dad continued his pace as he glanced inside. The room had decorated high-top tables as if for a reception. *Perhaps an afterparty.* If she could get in there, perhaps she would be able to see Lady Erica. They couldn't do it this early while the room looked empty; she and Dad would stand out, and there'd be questions. Maybe if they came back and timed it with the end of the fashion show, they could join the crowd. Haddie tugged Dad toward a mirror.

As she adjusted her too low neckline, she tilted her head. "I'm thinking that's being set up for an afterparty. Maybe we could get in there."

Taking her cue, he stepped up to the mirror and made as if to check his hair. "Perhaps. It could be another event entirely."

True. She didn't have any basis, more of a hope. Having Dad dig around the back halls seemed dangerous, so a safer path would be to stay together. "Okay. Let's take a lap around and see if we can get closer from another side, then come back. By then, maybe they'll have set up the table." Why would they need a table at an afterparty? *I might be rationalizing.*

As they turned for the arch, a coerced stepped through. A woman with large eyes and a pink jacket stopped and appraised them. The yellow haze wound through her face like tiny lightning bugs. "Saints, yes!" she exclaimed.

Haddie's chest tightened, expecting an attack. However, the woman seemed pleased, not aggressive. A young man with a top knot followed, striking a pose behind the dark-haired woman with his finger to his chin.

"Tall as a redwood. That perfect nose — a Greek

goddess." The woman approached to circle Haddie, examining every curve and feature.

Cheeks growing warm, Haddie raised her eyebrows, still too surprised to speak. She felt like one of Dad's prized antique bikes that some collector inspected.

"Yes. Yes. Yes, and yes. How did you hear about us?" The woman fluttered her hands in the air. "Social media, of course. Seth is a maestro. You're early, but that's a great sign. Follow. We'll get you a form to fill out." Striding toward the table, she turned and coaxed with her fingers. "Don't tell me you're shy. How cute. We'll get rid of that, soon enough."

Dad nudged Haddie into motion, and she stepped toward the yellow-hazed woman. The coerced she'd dealt with had been angry and violent, except for Josh, of course. This woman seemed real. *That's unfair.* It wasn't the woman's fault she'd been coerced, yet she seemed to retain a personality that Haddie assumed would have been removed. Did the woman know? She dug into a box still on the hotel staff's cart and found a form.

"I'm Sandy. What's your name, Dear?" She handed over a form.

Haddie swallowed. "Hilda."

"Wonderful." Sandy found a pen in another box. "Now, take this inside and fill it out. We don't expect anyone else for an hour, but there's an open bar. Save yourself for the dinner tonight, though. Bring me the form when you're done, and I'll get your badge ready."

"Dinner?" Haddie asked.

"At the ranch. Didn't read the whole post, did you?" Sandy smiled broadly as she tapped the pen and form in Haddie's hand. "We'll take her bus out to the ranch where Lady Erica and the other models will host all the applicants.

Don't worry. You're my ringer. Poolside dinner. For now, get a few drinks into you, but not too many. Just enough to loosen that tongue a bit."

"We've got our own car, if it would help." Dad smiled after his offer.

Sandy shook her head. "Everyone takes the bus. No boyfriends, though. Sorry."

Staring at the glow buzzing through the woman's eyes and imagining traveling confined in a bus took Haddie's breath away. "This is my dad."

"Agent," Dad corrected.

Sandy smirked. "One of those. Okay, agents are allowed. You'll find Lady Erica generous, but hard working. If you're not ready to launch a career with some heavy runway time, this isn't for you."

"She's ready. Thank you, Sandy." He veered Haddie into the room.

A surprised male bartender and busboy looked up. Neither had been coerced. Haddie's heart still raced as Dad led them to the bar.

"Aquavit. Two Hearted Ale." He pulled out a five for the tip jar.

The bartender grimaced. "I don't have either of those, Sir. No beer or ale at all."

I'll get sick if I drink now. Haddie motioned toward the table. "Plain club soda. I'm going to go fill this out." She left him at the bar and walked toward one of the farther high tops. *I would love a chair.* There wasn't one in the room. Tables had been spread along one wall; perhaps they planned snacks at some point. Kiana and Dad had briefly discussed the recruiting as a ruse to get near the event, not to actually apply, but to get close to Lady Erica. *Too close.*

Going to the ranch was more than they'd intended.

Would there be some chance of isolating Lady Erica? Then what? She probably would have excessive security. Coerced. Maybe even demons. *What am I doing?* Haddie had to at least try, for Josh's sake. They'd have time to notify Kiana and Aaron about the change in plans.

Trembling, she pulled out her ID to spell Hilda's last name.

CHAPTER 27

HADDIE'S HAND touched the stiff hairs of the wig and stopped. She pushed the door open to the bathroom and found a small floral-scented apartment with a row of cushioned seats and sinks in the back. Around the corner, full doors built into pink and white tile walls led to enclosed stalls. They all had signs like an airplane bathroom, and all six were vacant. Picking one, she put her purse on a small shelf and worked the black dress over her hips. Instrumentals from sixties songs echoed outside her door. The toilet paper felt thick enough to write on.

Dad waited in the holding room along with two applicants who had arrived shortly after Haddie finished her paperwork. The two women looked to be friends and had been less then gracious in their glares.

Haddie checked her phone and sighed. *Still no signal.* She'd have to head back to the lobby with her stylized name tag stuck on her dress; at least she wouldn't have trouble getting back to Dad. At the sink, she grabbed one of the wrapped mints.

She headed past the main foyer where the coerced

man still guarded the double doors. The next hall branched to the right to a hall of doors. A larger junction had two main halls and an open sitting room. Luckily, a loud pair stepped in from a courtyard letting in the city noise. A man smoked outside. Spinning on her heels, she cut through the sitting room and made for the door where she found the short man vaping from some small device. He offered an eager smile, but she just gave him a nod and moved toward the opposite side, searching for her phone. The air had a cool chill to it, but the sun shone warm.

Kiana answered immediately, "All good?"

"Yes, I guess." Haddie glanced back at the man, not wanting to be heard. He sharply averted his gaze back out to the street. "Change in plans. We couldn't get near the show. I've applied to be one of her models. They're having a party at their ranch, and Dad hoped you'd follow our bus in the RAV4. Keep out of sight. Just back up."

Kiana took a moment to respond. "Is this wise? Couldn't we just all tail the bus together?"

"I think at this point, I'd cause more attention not going. Besides, I want to see her up close and this is my chance." *And if I don't like her, would it be easier when Dad kills her?* Dad had seemed to be okay with infiltrating the ranch. He hadn't discouraged the situation, and he could have.

"I'm going to ask Aaron to come."

"He won't," Haddie said a little too sharply. She had tried to accept his position, but each time it came up she resented that he wouldn't try to help Josh. It forced her here, wearing a tight black dress around the coerced. The man vaping on the patio headed back inside, leaving her alone.

"Thomas thinks this is a good idea?" In the background

of Kiana's phone, a door closed and then the sound of loud knocking came. The connection crackled as if fading.

"Yes," Haddie replied.

The phone distorted. *We'll lose the connection.* It only took a moment before the latch sounded.

"They've got a plan," Kiana said. Her voice came through louder as she moved her phone and spoke to Haddie. "I'm with Aaron."

"Don't bother." Haddie regretted the comment immediately and took a deep breath. She pressed her lips together and closed her eyes. *I only really need Kiana in this.* If they had to leave quickly, having a vehicle waiting would be important. Aaron wasn't necessary.

Muffled in the background, she could hear Kiana explaining. Aaron asked a question quickly. Haddie couldn't hear the answer.

Aaron laughed, perhaps too loud for Haddie's benefit. "No, I'll just leave now."

Kiana sighed. "I'll be there. How soon?"

Haddie shrugged to herself. "I'm guessing the show goes till 2:30 or 3:00, so you've got a bit."

"I'm going to do a lap to get a lay of the streets and look for the bus. When it takes off, I'll follow at a good distance and find a place to keep hidden during the party. I've got your back, Haddie."

"Thanks. We'll be careful."

Haddie hung up and checked her battery. Fifty-three percent. The prepaid phones didn't last very long. A couple came out, and she caught the swinging door to head back inside. Partially from the sun, but more from her growing stress, sweat threatened under her arms and between her breasts. The air inside chilled her and smelled floral, more artificial than from the fresh flowers spilling out of the vases.

The traffic in the halls lessened after the fashion show got underway. The same coerced man waited at the doorway, and the temptation to flourish her sticker and beg for a peek faded as the yellow glow about his face became more evident. *What nest am I heading into?* Would Lady Erica attempt to coerce all the new model applicants once she had them at her ranch? Sameedha had affected a large group. Could Lady Erica?

The sight of two non-coerced attendants at Sandy's recruitment table calmed some concerns. Two well-dressed, petite young women joked and chatted as if they did this job regularly. If Haddie could check the models for coercion, she'd be more comfortable. It had sounded like Lady Erica and the other models would be escorting the new applicants to the ranch. If it looked dangerous, if all the models were coerced, then Haddie could feign an excuse not to go. Besides, she'd have found out everything she needed to know. *Except how to save Josh.*

Sandy waved fingers at Haddie as she passed. More applicants had joined the group so that six women had paired up around the room, none with their dads or agents.

"That took a while," Dad said.

He'd gotten her a fresh club soda, and she took a sip, looking at the closest pair. "No cell service inside. Kiana will be there."

"Aaron?"

Haddie snorted. "What do you think?"

Dad rubbed back his hair. "He's leaving."

"Yes."

"He's as smart as I give him credit for. This isn't his fight. It may end up being his fight, someday."

"The –" Haddie dropped her voice. "The demons were hunting him before us. It is his fight. He just runs."

Dad nodded. "Smart man. He has that choice. So do you. So do I. I initially chose that option, but this time I'm heading into the battle. Those are the choices in a war."

Haddie huffed, but she couldn't argue the point. She knew it, intellectually. It all boiled down to Josh. *I just wanted Aaron to take one small risk.*

The club soda must have been sitting for a while, as it had turned somewhat watery and flat. A wide-eyed woman entered with hair as blonde as Haddie's wig. Her round face with a button nose reminded Haddie of Liz for a quick moment. Behind her a young man strode in and rested his hand on her shoulder as the woman paused, looking at everyone. She swallowed and seemed nervous. He squeezed her shoulders and whispered something in her ear that made her smile. The way he did it reminded Haddie of David.

She could have chosen to skip the fashion show and meet with David. *Patch things up.* He knew when to make little jokes that would wash away the stress of her day or hold her hand when they sat in a coffee shop, so that she knew she was important to him. He'd curl up behind her in bed and listen to her concerns about work or her doubts about becoming a lawyer. He hadn't judged her or tried to fix her, he just listened. His only problem had been her secrets, and she still didn't dare tell him — drag him into her mess. Haddie turned her head so she couldn't watch the lovers. *I want that again.* She understood what her dad had tried to explain.

Three more women joined the applicants in the next few minutes. Haddie considered running to the bathroom, more out of nerves than from what she'd drank.

When a service door opened in the back of the room, heads turned at the noise.

The glimpse of a yellow glow showed through the wall, but Lady Erica stepped in alone and paused, scanning the room with her impressive stature and height. She wore a shiny black jacket over a pinkish-beige shirt that ruffled along the lapel and cuffs. The blouse seemed to have only one button fastened, just below the bustline so that Lady Erica's white-painted skin looked like an undergarment. She wore long pink hair, blood red lipstick, and red rimmed glasses that crossed her dark eyebrows. Her skirt looked like the same shiny material as the long jacket, perhaps silk.

The room turned silent as she waited, and the one coerced hid in the hallway beyond the door. As she finally strolled toward the center of the room, a line of models streamed in behind her. They likely wore what they'd just displayed for the show. The outfits ranged from garish to understated, both styles that Haddie found difficult to appreciate. Hardly important. *They aren't coerced.*

The sole coerced member strode in last, and he stood by the door with a tablet in hand. Unlike the previous coerced she'd met, he displayed calm patience. It seemed that those who served Lady Erica didn't act as guards so much as attendants.

Lady Erica raised both of her hands, covered in black gloves. "Welcome to Lady Erica's coterie, at least for the evening. Some of you will be chosen to join us. Present yourselves with poise and grace. This afternoon we will mingle, eat, and drink. I will have the opportunity to talk with all of you. Follow me now, to the bus and to the ranch."

With a flourish, she turned and strode back toward the service entrance. The models, both men and women, separated, as if rehearsed, to form a path for her. The coerced followed close behind Lady Erica, and then the models dropped in as if choreographed. *None of the models had been coerced.* If Dad had intended to break his word, this could have been the place and time. Haddie expected that the ranch would be guarded and controlled by Lady Erica. Sandy had entered at some point and waved the applicants to follow. Everyone had to take the bus and leave their cars behind.

In all, they'd only found three coerced. Not overwhelming evidence that Lady Erica was the coercer. The applicant ruse had been necessary. They might have found more evidence if they'd continued hunting around the hotel, but it didn't seem likely. *Do I still hold some hope of forcing her to fix Josh?*

Haddie shook her head, turning to Dad as she noticed the young lovers separating. "Let's go," she said.

CHAPTER 28

AARON CLOSED HIS EYES. Kiana stood behind him at the door. The room seemed airless and small. *Why is it so difficult to leave?* The air conditioner churned, filling the silence with its musty air. *They are making a mistake.*

He never intended to be part of all this. Thomas had understood the risks. Kiana would run to be their backup. Aaron wouldn't. *I can't.* He could not take the chance that danger would force him into using his power. In all these years, it had only been around Haddie that he had ever come close. The ski lift. Boise. *She is dangerous for me.* Still, the desire to know froze him. He ached to get into that car with Kiana, just to witness; he did not intend to jump into the fight.

"You don't have to leave. Just wait here. I'll be fine alone." Kiana sounded calm and understanding.

Her voice jerked him back into motion and he slid his laptop into its sleeve. He had to get away. Far from the temptation. "I have to go."

"I want to thank you, for Boise," she said. "I don't want you to leave thinking I didn't appreciate your help."

Aaron almost turned to see if she teased him, but her tone did not have that bite of sarcasm. "Thank me?"

"You emptied your gun, drew their attention. You might have even hit one of them; I couldn't tell — running for my life. You stood in the open and took careful shots. I mentioned it once and you dismissed it."

The bullets from Barbara's men had been whizzing by him. The muzzles seemed to flare directly at him. It had been careless of him to even try and help. He had nearly used his powers in that moment when the gun clicked empty. *I almost shouted for them to stop.* If he had, it all would have turned out differently. Instead, Haddie, Kiana, and Thomas had taken care of everything. "Okay," he said. Taking a deep breath, he coiled up his laptop cord. "I am still leaving."

"I understand. I don't know what burns at you deep inside, but I can respect it."

Aaron drew in a breath. *What does she suspect?* "What do you mean?"

"There's a terror that grips you sometimes. Not always when we talk about getting near demons or coerced, sometimes it seems to haunt you from the past. Then, there's something about Haddie's coworker, Josh. It gives me the creeps, but there's something more in it for you."

He could feel his pulse increase. She did not know about his ability, or she hid it well, but she had gauged his reactions correctly. "It is personal," he said, before he could deny it.

"I guessed it was. I don't mean to pry. I just wanted to acknowledge that you've been an important part of our group these past few weeks. I didn't want to dismiss it. Thanks again, for Boise."

He tucked the cords into his bag and tried to breathe

away the tension. Now that Haddie knew his secret, he would always feel exposed. It had been a mistake to tell her. *I did not intend it.* His best choice would be to leave and continue on his own.

Kiana's phone rang, and he started slightly. A muffled voice came from the phone. "Haddie?" she asked.

He turned.

Kiana's face pinched and she pressed into the phone as if she couldn't hear. "Wait, what? What about Thomas?" Kiana bustled past him toward the window of the room. "Say that again."

Kiana leaned against the window, pulled back, and swore. She began dialing a number.

Something had happened. Something that would beg him to get involved. *I won't.* With an annoyed tone he asked, "What?"

CHAPTER 29

Thomas stepped onto a large tour bus that smelled of perfume and disinfectant. Haddie walked a step ahead and paused for the line that had already formed between the seats. The middle-aged driver smiled briefly but checked the mirror to watch the clamoring crowd growing in the back of the bus. Lady Erica had boarded ahead of them with the coerced man who clung to a black tablet. Sandy, her face buzzing with coercion, stood at the door to the bus, urging them on with pleasant comments. He didn't spot any guards or guns. *Only two coerced.* The line moved in a slow crawl, pausing at each step.

Passing the driver, he found two women blocking Haddie.

"No phones on the ranch, Honey." Thin faced, the woman smiled and gestured to a Ziploc that the other woman held up. "You'll get them tonight when the bus comes back to the hotel."

Haddie glanced back and then handed in her phone.

Thomas let the woman repeat her request as Haddie

waited for him just ahead. The bus would be crowded. "Why?" he asked.

The woman's smile shifted, forced. "Models. Pool party. Everyone needs to feel comfortable that there won't be any pictures going out to the media."

He doubted the excuse. Thomas shrugged. "Of course, understand." He pulled out his phone and noticed a missed call from an unknown number. He considered stepping away and listening, but the line had quickly piled behind him, and Haddie seemed nervous. *Likely spam.* He handed over his phone.

The other woman wrote "TJ" on the Ziploc and dropped it into a box.

The seats rippled and wove down the sides in a curving pattern that hid the boxy shape of the bus. Lady Erica, easily identifiable by her height and bright pink hair, sat in the back on a bench with her short, dark-haired attendant. Most of the models sat along the sides, but some stood in the aisles talking.

Haddie waited, obviously uncomfortable. Thomas smiled and motioned toward a space along the seats for them to sit. "This is interesting," he said.

Forcing a smile she nodded, then a second time toward the opposite side near the front of the bus. He saw only a young applicant who couldn't be older than eighteen. The movement of the glow behind her made him focus. Four distinct coerced moved outside the bus, splitting into pairs and traveling away. Lady Erica's attendant and Sandy outside made six. "Interesting." He shifted to turn toward Haddie and checked the area behind their seats. Clear.

Haddie focused on the four glows ahead of them. "I think they're getting into cars. Escorts?" She spoke softly, but he could hear her over the racket.

"Perhaps." Glancing over at the two women collecting phones, he could see Sandy's glow. "Another," he said quietly. A yellow haze moved past Sandy, heading into the bus.

The last of the applicants on board, the two women stored the phones in a cabinet overhead and then sat close to the front. The coerced man who had been checking invitations walked past Thomas and Haddie to stand in the back, closer to Lady Erica.

Sandy followed, smiling at her applicants and talking with one of the models ahead of her in the bus.

The four outside remained in pairs, close enough that they might be sitting in vehicles. Seven coerced so far. Enough evidence that Lady Erica was likely the coercer. However, getting an inside glimpse into her security would be priceless when setting up someone to track her. He hadn't seen her use a phone yet, but her attendant carried that tablet with care. *He has to sleep sometime.*

Thomas turned back toward the front and found a last coerced climbing up the steps. Nudging Haddie, Thomas tensed. Behind were two demons. The bright orange eyes gleamed. The coerced man with a trimmed goatee stepped in and stood nearly in front of them, grasping one of the support straps from the ceiling. The demons dressed in dark suits, which made them look like security. Their faces expressionless, they stopped near the driver. They blocked the exit. None seemed to have guns. Demons wouldn't need them.

What do they look like under that disguise? Haddie had described the ones she'd seen, and he'd had his first encounter in Boise.

Haddie gripped his arm.

Stay calm. The woman sitting next to him, an applicant

he recognized from the waiting room, adjusted her top and gave him a dour look.

Thomas smiled, staring ahead at the blinds that covered the far windows. In his peripheral vision he could see the demons, but they seemed to settle in for the ride as the driver closed the door. The lights turned off in the bus, high-lighting the coerced and demons. Haddie gripped tighter.

Lights flickered on under the seats, and colored rails lit the passengers in rainbow colors. One of the coerced pairs outside pulled away. *Definitely a vehicle. Eight coerced. Two demons.* There might be more at the ranch. His and Haddie's ruse had proven to be a risky encounter, but unless they brought attention to themselves, they should be safe. He had solid information for anyone he would assign to track Lady Erica. If only Haddie didn't have to be exposed to the danger as well.

The bus lurched into motion, and the two women who had collected cell phones got up to retrieve drinks for the passengers. Sandy walked down the aisle, chatting and trailing a hand along the colored rails. Eventually she came to them. "Don't be nervous," she said to Haddie. "You'll be fine."

Thomas patted Haddie's hand. "She's good. So, how far away is this ranch?"

"An hour. We'll be there in time to get you settled into the dining room. The models will meet us for the pool party afterward."

He considered asking about the security at the front of the bus; it should be noticeable to anyone on board, but it wouldn't gather any useful information. "I didn't bring a suit."

Sandy smiled. "Lady Erica provides all. Besides, it gets chilly quick in the mountains."

"Mountains?"

"Diablo range. It's beautiful." She smiled at Haddie. "From San Francisco?"

Haddie shook her head. "Washington."

Sandy frowned slightly. "How'd you end up at the recruitment? And so quickly? You were early. Seth only sets up the ads to the local community."

Thomas tensed. They hadn't even considered setting their back story very deep.

Looking down, Haddie acted embarrassed. "I follow the fashion magazines; they mentioned that you sometimes do recruitments." She peeked up, as if checking to see that Sandy wasn't mad. "We just took a chance and drove down here."

"All the way from Washington?" Sandy shook her head. "Well perseverance more than makes up for your age."

On the form, they'd put Haddie down as twenty-one, the age on her license. Was that old for models? Haddie had her mother's bones and always looked younger than she was.

"I hope so," Haddie said. "Will we be doing auditions tonight?"

Sandy shook her head. "Lady Erica likes to meet applicants as people first. Then she'll let me know if I should gather a portfolio and see if the experience is there. Don't worry about all that, just be natural." She moved across the aisle to one of the other applicants.

One of the women who had taken their phones followed with drinks, not at all surprised when he and Haddie picked club soda.

Haddie spoke, lips on her drink. "This ought to be interesting. I'm glad we fueled up before San Francisco."

Thomas kept a smile on his face. Kiana would be

following, and an hour's drive wouldn't eat up much gas, so she wouldn't lose them. He wished he could warn her about the coerced that escorted the bus. Hopefully she'd catch that right away. If anything went wrong, Lady Erica had more forces than they could handle. *Nothing should go wrong.* He took a deep breath and glanced toward the front. The demons remained focused and vigilant. Under the ties of their jackets, he could see a faint yellow glow. Haddie had mentioned their medallions. She had made a medallion disappear to unleash one of them. Inside this bus, it would be a slaughter. Still, he'd keep it in mind if he needed it. For now, he smiled and sipped his club soda.

CHAPTER 30

HADDIE STEPPED off the bus without focusing on the rows of grape vines or the mountains, instead positioning the coerced and demons around her. Beyond the smell of heat and oil drifting from under the bus, the air had an earthy scent from the plantings. The bus parked on a lot at the foot of a slope of vineyard that extended from the front of the house. The driveway continued along the left side under large oaks to a building, likely a garage. A forested mountain ridge crested behind the house and to her right on the west side. Below and to the left, it sloped sharply into a valley.

Two of the coerced had driven to the top of the driveway in a white Ford Expedition. She'd lost their haze but could see the top of their car. The other two parked behind the bus; she could see their glows. Sandy and Lady Erica's other assistants had escorted her off first. The two demons waited by the fenced-in vineyard in front of the house. Haddie hung back with Dad near the bus while the models circled the pink-haired Lady Erica.

Behind the woman to the north above the ridge, white clouds stretched across a bright blue sky. In the sunlight, her painted skin looked alien, and the slick satin cr silk added to the effect.

"Welcome, everyone. This is one of my favorite getaways here in northern California. The pool is down there," she indicated downslope to the east, behind the bus, "but we'll be enjoying a meal at the house first, where I hope to get to know everyone a little more intimately before we move to the pool to join the coterie for a party. Suits are available for those who want to brave the evening's chill air. Follow me."

She turned and led the way, her short, tablet-carrying coerced hurrying to keep up with her long strides. Her other two attendants followed ahead of the models; Sandy led the applicants, walking backward at one point to urge them on. The squat house stretched across the top of the hill above, with chimneys dotting the roof and a porch that wrapped around it. A white picket fence separated the driveway from the house. Unnaturally green grass circled the building.

Haddie and Dad kept to the back of the group, where the two demons watched everyone. She expected them to attack. They had no emotion to their faces. Were they even close to human as Liz and Aaron suggested? Mutants of some sort? What did they think? She waited until she'd climbed the driveway a little bit before turning. They remained below but watched her. The clouds over the bus looked like a storm far to the southern horizon. Would they end the party early if the weather moved in?

The mountains loomed around the building, which lay in a flat hollow beside a ridge that ran west and south around it. The road they'd come up wove through oaks and pines into a northern valley, and the infinity pool hung over the sharper edge of a valley to the east. Buildings dotted the red-bricked patio of the pool. If they had to escape, the only easy way out was down the road.

Bulbs dangled from a pole at the top row of the vineyard and hung over the grapevines near the front of the house. Every other post along the white picket fence had small lights as well, though nothing was lit except for the house. At the top of the driveway a flagpole stood empty. *Why call this a ranch?*

The white Expedition had been left in front of the garage, and Haddie thought she picked up the guards' glows deeper in the house. The structure extended into the backyard from the west end, forming a corner. Dark windows dotted the wall ahead of them, and the extension ended near a small oak. The parade of people crossed a manicured lawn, passed under a section of the porch that seemed to wrap around the entire house, and entered the back doors in the center of the building at the corner.

Inside the house, warm lights had already been lit in most of the rooms. When they entered, Sandy led the applicants through a beautifully tiled house with expansive rooms and high ceilings with exposed beams. They stopped where a long row of pale, wooden tables stretched in front of warm flames crackling in the fireplace. A spicy Mexican dish dominated the air, but a taint of death scented the room as well, like spoiled meat. Lady Erica sat at the end of the table, and her short attendant stood near the door behind her.

The sound of dishes and pans carried from around the corner. Sandy pointed to seats at the table, tapping the backs of chairs to encourage everyone to find a place.

Haddie marked two coerced in the kitchen and two more in a room at the back of the house. *We're surrounded.* Dad, glancing at the scant decor, seemed to be checking the guards' positions. He picked a pair of seats near the middle with their backs to the fire. She could see into part of the kitchen, where the coerced who had been manning the door and the other with the goatee helped prepare trays.

Lady Erica sat tall and calm, waiting for everyone to find a seat. Like Haddie and her dad, like Sameedha and Barbara, and even Harold Holmes, each person with power had been nearly six feet tall. All except for the short man, Araki, who had made the earth move, crushed the investigator in Boise, and nearly killed them with flying boulders. Did height have some connection? It had to. Some genetic aspect. *Liz will love this.*

After filling Lady Erica's goblet, Sandy silently took carafes of red and white wine and began walking around offering to fill glasses. The room hushed, allowing the noise of the kitchen to dominate. When everyone had chosen, Sandy headed into the kitchen and Lady Erica raised her glass. "To the coterie," she toasted.

Haddie joined the others, repeating the toast before taking a small sip. Wine had never been a favorite of hers, but during the toast, she had the opportunity to note what she could of Lady Erica and her assistants. It seemed they hurried to whatever task needed done, unlike the quiet lurker who waited with the tablet. Did he only have one function? He held the device carefully, almost reverently. Is that how the leader contacted Lady Erica? The more she watched the man, the surer she became. It would matter in the end, but for now they just needed to observe. Dad's people could focus on the man and his tablet.

As Sandy and the other two coerced came out with trays of appetizers, Lady Erica waved an indolent finger around the group. "We'll go around the table. Tell me your passions. What brings you here to this meal?"

Haddie's chest grew tight as Lady Erica motioned to the first woman and the applicant nervously stumbled through an attempt to sound altruistic in her interests. The others around the table glazed as well, and few noticed their plates. Dad ate heartily. Haddie hadn't planned on giving a speech. *I knew I'd have to talk. Relax, Haddie.* She took a breath and formulated what she could into a cohesive lie. The last thing she'd ever be interested in would be modeling, but she'd picked a legal career and wasn't very successful, at least not as an intern. Classes had gone well, despite a few missed papers around the Harold Holmes' incident.

Models, dressed in bathing suits and cover ups, passed quietly at the end of the room, heading to the pool.

Idly taking a bite of her appetizer, she found a salty and spicy anchovy inside the deep-fried ball. It wasn't bad, just unexpected. The next speaker had begun, a bit smoother than the first, though no one except Lady Erica seemed to be paying attention. Some looked terrified. Haddie had less to worry about. She needed to sound authentic, but didn't have the pressure of a potential callback for a deeper inter-view, though a plot did dance at the outer edge of her thoughts about getting Lady Erica alone during that process. Dad would likely not allow it. She doomed Josh by not having a better plan. Somehow, chipper little Sandy seemed to retain some inherent personality, which gave her some hope that Liz's theory might be true. If — when — Dad killed Lady Erica, Josh might be free.

She reached for her water and noticed the two glows from the back trailing toward the kitchen. *The guards are moving.* Nudging Dad with her elbow, she continued to sip the water. The speaker hardly noticed their focus, and Lady Erica nibbled an anchovy while she listened.

Sandy and the other coerced in the kitchen moved

bowls onto trays, readying the next course. The two guards moved as though in unison and came to a stop in the middle of the kitchen. One peered around the corner, and Haddie watched him over her glass. He stared, so she put it down to trade for another bite of the anchovy appetizer. *They're looking directly at us.* The guard glanced at a phone and then motioned to the unseen coerced by his side. The two hurriedly retraced their steps. *Did they recognize us — perhaps Dad?* Did the leader of the Unceasing, the one who had sent the letter, know what Dad looked like?

Tilting his head down, Dad wiped a non-existent smudge off his jacket. "Cough, choke," he directed in a whisper. He must have thought they'd been identified. Dad had a plan.

Gracelessly, Haddie sprayed the table with an anchovy cough. She followed with raucous hacking. The woman on the other side of the table yelped. Whining, she wiped her arm in a frenzy. All eyes turned to Haddie and Dad. Sandy stepped out from the kitchen with a quizzical look.

Dad stood up, thumping Haddie's back. "Bathroom?" he asked a startled Sandy. She pointed to the back.

Were the guards getting weapons? Confirming with the leader? Haddie stood, napkin to her face. Blood pounded in her ears. They'd escape down the hill and find Kiana. *Out a bathroom window in this dress?* Heart pounding, Haddie let Dad lead her out of the dining room.

CHAPTER 31

Haddie's pulse raced. Dad led them around the corner like he knew the building. Her heels clattered on the tile, and she could hear Lady Erica's voice asking someone a question. The yellow haze of the two guards showed through the walls. They had stopped. The other glowing coerced clustered in the kitchen behind them but still shifted as though working on the meal.

Dad spun at the end of a hall with a bathroom off to one side. Across, two bedroom doors were open, and clothes from the models littered the beds. *This is a dead end. No doors. Just windows.*

Haddie heard a song build and ring out. *It sounds like mine.*

"Did you hear that?" she asked. Had that been Lady Erica's tone? Someone had just used a power. Before, others had sounded different from Haddie's own. Even Dad's. Was there someone like her here? They'd assumed Lady Erica to be the only one. Had this been a trap?

Dad gestured for her to be quiet, then he entered one of the rooms. Two beds, made up like couches, lined each wall with a small end table between them. Gaudy outfits from the fashion show were piled on top of covers and pillows. Windows at the head of each bed framed the lawn and picket fence.

After a glance down the hall, Haddie followed.

Lady Erica yelled something from the dining area. Her tone sounded both concerned and commanding. Chairs scraped against floors. A metal pan or tray hit tile in the kitchen. All the sounds echoed in a jumble through the house. Boots thudded on the floor.

Through the walls, she could see the glows of the coerced shifting. The guards were moving in their tight pair toward Haddie. Those she imagined with Sandy remained clustered in one spot. Protecting Lady Erica? There were too many coerced, too many demons.

Dad ran to a bedroom window, unlocked it, and slid it open. "Out."

Haddie moved forward, grabbed the hem of her skirt, and yanked it up over her hips. There was no way she'd get over a bed and out a window otherwise. The clothes she climbed over seemed damp.

We need to make it to Kiana. Too many coerced filled the property. Even if they used their abilities, she and Dad would be overpowered. Escape was their only option. There had only been a long, wooded road up the mountainside to the house. *Surely, Kiana parked along there.*

On this side of the building, just past the lawn and white picket fence, a slope climbed into the trees, higher into the mountain. A small building nestled in the woods, and a path led to it. Toward the back of the lawn, a white stairway cut from the grass through the fence to the trail. Haddie ran for the stairs, holding the black dress at her thighs. Kiana would be down the mountain to their right, but so would the two coerced waiting by the bus and the two demons. They had to get away first, then they could circle back to Kiana.

Stepping off the porch, Haddie's heels sunk into the pungent grass, and she kicked them off mid-stride. Dad caught her arm as she struggled to catch her balance. The dress made things worse.

From somewhere downhill, past the vineyards, the same song as before started and rang out. Instinctively, Haddie growled her protective tone that enabled her to resist others' powers. *Who is that?* Lady Erica could not have made it down there. *There's someone else.*

A gunshot cracked. Birds in the woods flapped through trees, crying as they went. Dad turned and growled, his tone ringing in the air.

Haddie spun too late. Whoever had fired was gone. The open window she'd climbed through stood empty. The other rooms had lights on, but nothing moved. Voices called from down the hill, beyond the vineyard. The birds seemed louder than any of the other noises. *We've got to get to Kiana.*

Dad sagged. Blue mist trailed off his neck and face. Likely he relived the visions that came with using their powers.

We've got to go. Reaching out to steady him, she turned back toward the house at a movement. A shadow shifted in the room she'd escaped. A glow showed there. When the guard jumped to the window opposite the open one, Haddie sang. His gunshot clapped the air. The muzzle flashed. Glass shattered from the window. He faded.

Dad grunted and fell out of her grasp. She felt a spray of blood on her cheek as her skin burned from using her powers. *He's been hit.* Sucking in a breath from her pain, she swayed before the visions took her.

The grass and house faded into darkness. The air smelled like salt water and blood. The ship's cabin had barely a sliver of moonlight reflected off clouds outside the porthole. An engine thrummed, vibrating through everything. The bed rocked with the waves. Her shoulder burned where the knife pulled out. The man, no more than a shadow, lifted his arm to stab again, and she sang out.

The night noise of automobiles and a city sounded down an alley behind her. Windows three stories up lit the brick walls on opposite sides. Trash rotted in fetid heaps. Two men kicked a third on the ground. "Hey," she yelled, hearing her dad's gruff voice. They turned, aiming a black pistol that reflected a glimmer off its barrel from the windows above. She growled, and the two men were gone.

Bright light splashed into her eyes as it reflected off the snow. Shot, her horse cried out and stumbled, pulling at the harness and teetering the cart. Laura screamed, leaning against the tilt, and held tighter to their swaddled baby in her arms. *My wife, my child.* Ahead in the forest, the two men stepped from behind the pines. They vanished with Haddie's growl.

The blue and white sky of the ranch returned, and Haddie staggered barefoot in the grass. Only moments had passed during the visions. *We're too exposed here.* Dad had dropped to a knee. His black suit hid the bullet wound for a second, then she saw wet cloth in his left armpit. Her own skin burning, she grabbed under his right arm. "We've got to run." Her joints ached at every move. His would too.

He nodded, leaning into her grip to rise from his knee. *How bad was the gunshot wound?*

Downhill, Haddie heard crashing through the vineyard.

The song had come from down there. Dad leaned into her as she twisted to see behind her. The bus started, then ground into gear. The vines moved. She could see the orange glow of the demon's eyes before it leaped over the grapes into sight.

The raw red flesh of its head seemed little more than a bud on the stalk of its long neck. Mouth and nose seemed to merge into a slit between its eyes. Its arms ended in long black nails that curved down like a praying mantis. Slashing and hopping, it raced toward them. Between each row, it disappeared. Where was the other demon?

"Hell," Dad croaked.

The grotesque creature bobbed up from the vines, slashing.

I need to stop it. Her mind and body flinched at the thought. Her skin still felt flayed off her bones from her last episode. Haddie drew in a deep breath.

Dad growled and his song rung the air. The demon's head had just appeared in a mist of red that hung over the top of green vines, then it faded, turning porous and vanishing.

The sounds of screams joined the grinding gears of the bus. Something was happening down at the driveway and the pool.

He sagged against her. We've got to get away. There were too many coerced, and another demon.

"C'mon, Dad." She leaned into him and got under his arm. He flinched at her grasp. She knew the pain he felt on his skin. *I can't help it.* They had to get to the woods. To Kiana. They never should have come, not after they saw how many coerced were guarding Lady Erica. Not after the demons.

He managed a step, then another toward the white

stairs. They had to get to the woods. He wasn't moving fast enough. The other guards likely had guns as well. *I don't see the other demon.* Perhaps it rampaged down below. *We need a break.*

"Stop." Lady Erica sang from behind them.

CHAPTER 32

Haddie's protective tone wavered under the force of Lady Erica's song. A cloying draw tugged at Haddie. Lady Erica's note rebounded, but not the way Sameedha's had felt.

Dad fell out of her hands and landed on his knees with one hand in the grass.

Haddie turned to find Lady Erica standing at the front corner of the house under the overhang of the porch. Her stark white skin seemed a sharp contrast to her shiny outfit. Light blue mist trailed from her shoulders and through pink hair. Her arm twitched, but she didn't seem to sag or stumble with the effort of using her power.

Haddie snarled back and felt her tone rebuffed without effort. "Dad." She reached her hand back to grab him.

He clawed at his face, as if trying to remove the yellow haze that now lay across his eyes.

"No!" yelled Haddie. Her tone rang out, rebuked. Instinctively, she'd attempted her protective song on him. It had worked with Barbara. During the attack. Not after. *I'm too late.* If she'd been warned, she might have saved him.

Lady Erica sang out again, "Kill her. Destroy her."

Haddie barely strengthened her defenses before the power of Lady Erica's song knocked her back a step.

Falling flat to the grass, Dad shook as though he had a seizure.

Haddie hung onto her song, weathering Lady Erica's tone. *This isn't happening.* "Dad?"

The haze clung to him — taking her Dad from her. Did he fight against it?

Wielding kitchen knives, Sandy and the other coerced rounded the front of the house toward them. New glows lit up inside the house. Lady Erica had coerced the other applicants.

Dad whimpered from the ground. "Run." The haze clung to his face.

I'm too tired. She ached from using her power. Her skin chafed under the dress. It felt as though her face peeled. *I can't leave him.*

The coerced man with the goatee raced across the lawn toward her. He gripped a short steak knife. His face screwed into an enraged grimace. Haddie almost let down her guard to attack him. Sandy and the man who'd been collecting invitations weren't far behind him. Lady Erica waited patiently at the corner of the house. *I'm going to kill her. It might free Dad.* If Haddie tried to use her power on the other coerced, Lady Erica would coerce her. Haddie might be able to fight off one of the coerced, but not all three.

The man with the tablet stepped around the corner of the house and raised a gun.

Haddie flinched at the gunshot, then hiked her skirt. *I'm sorry, Dad.*

She ran for the white stairs in a crouch. As the coerced fired another bullet, she zigged and zagged her course. After the third gunshot, she reached the stairs. The fence to the right side splintered with a fourth shot. *Horrible aim.*

The ridiculous dress bunched in her hands, she bent over and climbed, waiting for a bullet to hit her. Birds ahead still cried out. Far away, the bus ground gears. Someone screamed downhill, and Haddie imagined it to be the models. She padded up the wooden steps, feeling trapped as the gunshots continued.

Someone behind her grunted. Haddie stumbled on the last step, bracing against the wood with her spare hand. Stones bit into the bottoms of her feet as she scrambled. A bullet thudded into a tree.

When she turned onto the brick pavers, she could see her pursuers. The man with the goatee climbed the stairs. Blood dripped from his leg. Had he been shot? Sandy and the other coerced had almost reached the stairs.

Dad still writhed on the grass.

Lady Erica waited at the corner of the house. She watched with a sense of calmness that mocked Haddie's scrambling escape. The man who fired at Haddie still gripped his tablet. One of the applicants, the young lover, staggered onto the porch behind Lady Erica. The coercion process seemed to debilitate the victims, at least at first.

The bricks scraped the pads of Haddie's feet. After using her powers, her skin felt raw. The man fired again, his bullet rustling into the woods.

Ahead, the small building nestled under the trees looked like a chapel. Large oaks spread above, offering cool shade. The mountain ridge rose on her left. She imagined that if she ran straight, the forest would slope down to the road where Kiana waited. *Then what?*

Lady Erica had coerced Dad. *I can't leave him here.*

Kiana would have brought a weapon. They would come back and force the woman to free Dad.

Haddie ran under the tree on the far side of the chapel. The gunfire had stopped. Perhaps he'd run out of bullets. Shoes sounded on the paved trail behind her. Thin brush, bright green in the middle of summer, dotted the mountainside leading to the north. The shade cooled the air, and it smelled like mushrooms. Heart pounding with the escape, her chest grew tight as she left Dad lying on the grass under Lady Erica's grip. Leaves and mulch slid under her feet and stuck between her toes as she raced past the building.

The slope dropped sharply toward the vineyard to her right. The parking lot below had a black SUV parked there, but no sign of the other coerced guards or the other demon. On the opposite side of the drive, she could glimpse the empty pool area. *Where are the models?* Towels littered the red brick patio around the water, but she could not see one sign of a model.

Her view disappeared as trees downslope rose to dense tops of green leaves. Where was the other person who had sung? Lady Erica had another person with power here. *I'll have to deal with them too.* Barbara and Araki had worked together. Haddie didn't relish the idea of confronting someone else, but she wouldn't leave Dad.

Sandy, or the other coerced, had reached the woods beside the chapel. They crashed through the brush and leaves behind her. People still screamed below.

A single vine, sharp with thorns, rooted to her right and climbed through brush. It anchored around an oak to her left. It held firm as she ran into it, scraping down her right leg to her ankle. Yanking, as her left leg rose off the ground, Haddie tripped.

She almost caught her balance. The damnable dress

dropped out of her grasp, and as she rolled off her back, the hem wrapped tightly around her knees. The slope and momentum spun her into a sideways twirl. Her hands carefully blocking her face, she careened off a young sapling with her forearm.

Rolling twice, she picked up speed. Blue sky and forest shadows spun around her before she launched over a head-high drop. The tree above drifted slowly overhead as she hung in free fall. Bright green leaves filtered the sunlight.

She hit the slope with a jarring thud. Leaves shoved into her mouth as she sucked air back into her lungs. A trunk appeared and her heels slammed into it, tearing into her ankles and spinning her. The dress ripped up the right side and flapped at her hips. Hairs yanked as the wig twisted.

Any sense of direction disappeared except the knowledge that she tumbled downward. Her side slammed into another trunk, and she lost the ability to breathe. The impact spun her but didn't stop the fall. Curling into a ball from the pain, she plummeted blindly.

The white fence of the vineyard shattered like pins under a bowling ball. Wood splintered, scraping into her dress and skin. The soft earth flattened, absorbing her momentum. A stake snapped before she wound around a grapevine's trunk and came to a stop.

Haddie sucked in breaths. *They're right behind me.* She had to get up and move north toward the road, toward Kiana. After all the crashing, the vineyard seemed silent. Her elbow pressed into the soil, but managed to push her face up. The dress draped loosely on her left side. Torn from hem to armpit, it left her right side exposed. Scratches covered her legs and arms. Her left side felt like there might be broken ribs.

She sat up and pressed her palms into soil. Sandy and

the invitation-collecting coerced climbed carefully down the hillside. They were far back by the chapel where the slope didn't run as steep.

Haddie eased herself to her feet and turned north. The white fence came to a corner close to where she crashed through. She stood at the last row of vines. The parking lot and an empty, black Ford Expedition waited just on the other side of the white pickets. *I need to get to Kiana.* Untangling from the stake and twine, she considered the possibility that the vehicle might have keys left in it. Where had the two coerced security guards gone? The other demon?

Wincing, she hobbled toward the fence where she'd smashed through.

CHAPTER 33

Haddie stepped over the broken wood, careful not to tear the soles of her feet anymore than they already were. In her panicked run, she'd found twigs and thorns on the forest floor. Sandy and the other coerced still had a way to climb down, but once they got to level ground, they had shoes. Haddie could run downhill, hoping to find where Kiana parked, but the Ford made more sense. She ran, grateful for the grass. The pavement she ran toward looked smooth from a distance.

Please have keys. She'd hotwired cars before, but only in the garage. If she took the time to try it, Sandy would be on her. *I don't want to kill her.* Sandy had as little choice in this as Josh did, or Dad.

What would Haddie do if she had to face Dad? She had already tried to push the coercion out of him. *I don't know how.* If Aaron were here, she'd force him. *No more asking.* Could she send Kiana back for Aaron? He might have already left the hotel. *Isn't that what he threatened?* She clenched her hands as she reached the asphalt and stones bit into her feet. *Not smooth at all.* Angry, she winced and painfully jogged toward the vehicle. She couldn't see any sign of the two coerced guards or the demon. Only the soft haze of Sandy and the other coerced appeared behind her. Where was the other person who had sung?

Down the driveway, a white glimmer hung at the forest's edge. As she squinted, trying to focus, it disappeared as if a reflection. A light wind stroked the trees and caused movement in the shade. *I'm being paranoid.*

With her hand on the back of the SUV, she slowed. Haddie opened the driver's door. Her side screamed as she leaned in. There was no key in the ignition nor the tray. Her throat grew thick. *I'm not giving up.* Stumbling across the pavement, she made for the field that curved for a short bit along the drive. Thicker grass stalks stabbed into the bottom of her feet, more painful than the protruding gravel of the asphalt.

Sandy had reached the bottom of the incline, farther back from where Haddie had tumbled, and raced along the white picket fence toward the parking lot. Haddie ran for the drive, gritting her teeth at the pain. The other coerced still hadn't gotten out of the woods. She could kill Sandy and the other coerced, or try to run for it. *I'd never stay ahead of them, not for long, not barefoot* Haddie ran anyway. Hope that she could free Dad had withered. *I've lost.* Over the ridge of the paved parking lot another field of vineyards showed leafy tops strung between tall stakes. They sloped down and out of sight.

Along the west side of the road, a reflection lit up in the woods that crawled thick up the ridge. A circle of mist rolled in on itself. *A light?* Perhaps some lamp or marker for the road. *I've got to get to Kiana.*

Someone lying in the brush between two oaks waved at Haddie.

Her chest tightened with panic. *The other song?* Perhaps one of the models. She almost stopped running, but Sandy still followed. Even barefoot, Haddie had a longer stride.

She recognized Kiana's hair and beads, draped over half her face. Hidden in the shadows of the woods, she sat there, not even trying to get up. What had happened?

Sandy had almost reached the paved drive, so Haddie had a lead, but not for long. She raced into the woods toward Kiana.

"What happened?" she asked.

Kiana sat with her left leg extended and the other folded to the side. She frowned at the question. "Are you okay? It's broken. Why are you wearing the wig?"

How had Kiana broken her leg? And this close to the house? Haddie leaned down, palms to her knees. Her side ached from the bruise and running. "How? Where are you parked?" Haddie turned to watch Sandy run and shook her head. "Do you have your gun?" She would kill Sandy, if she had to, then shoot Lady Erica.

"Gun? Aaron has it. What's wrong, Haddie?" Kiana suddenly seemed suspicious. "Are you okay? Did you kill her? Where is Thomas?"

Kiana's tone made her seem confused. Sandy would be on them any moment. Haddie only had a couple seconds, but she had to tell her. "Lady Erica got to Dad. She coerced him."

"Yes, I know." Kiana leaned back, as if suddenly intimidated or cautious. "What is wrong with you, Haddie?"

"Did Aaron run away - take the RAV4?"

Kiana shook her head, swallowed, and just stared.

What is wrong with her?

Sandy only had a few more seconds before she would spot Kiana. *I've got to lead her away.*

"Wait here." Haddie raced across the road heading into the thin woods. The lower vineyard stretched at the base of a sharp slope. *Aaron is here.* She had a chance to save Dad. Had Aaron actually gone up to the house to help? Her feet barely registered the leaves and twigs.

Haddie curved her path in the woods as she headed toward the parking lot and the Ford. Sandy arced to intercept her. The coerced woman glanced back once toward Kiana's location. Had Sandy seen Kiana? *I'm going to have to hurt her.* She didn't want to, but what choice did she have? At least the woman had been diverted and chased Haddie instead of attacking Kiana. How had she broken her leg?

The other coerced who had been taking invitations crossed over the parking lot and angled to pen Haddie in. He would block her path back to the driveway, and she had to get to the house. *Find Aaron. Get to Dad.* She could turn and run through the vineyard, but it would lead her east, toward the pool. The short man didn't hold the knife well. Haddie pivoted and raced toward him. Her feet were deadened from running, so she barely felt the stalks or twigs unless they hit inside her arch.

The man, red-faced from running, slowed as he realized she ran toward him. The yellow haze hung off his eyes. He pushed his arm out wide, preparing to slash. Coming to a complete stop, he waited for her, taking deep, ragged breaths. Sandy followed; Haddie wouldn't have much time. *I won't kill them.* Like her dad and Josh, they had no choice. She had to disable them.

Haddie slowed to a stop. She'd never physically attacked someone before, outside of sparring. Her neck chilled and the torn dress seemed to let in a cool breeze. *What am I doing?*

The man lunged, attempting to slash at her stomach. She swept his knife hand to the side and caught his wrist. With a twist and a palm to his shoulder, she sent him face first into the grass.

She pinned him with a knee in his back. Reacting with instinct, her training flowed in her movements. Her side throbbed, nearly taking her breath away. Using both hands, she pinned his arm and the steak knife into the grass. He struggled, uncoordinated and untrained. The yellow haze over his hidden eyes wove like insects, the lights visible through the back of his skull. He didn't choose to do this. *I can't hurt him.* Slowly, she pried the weapon away and tossed it far into the tall grass.

Haddie jumped off him as Sandy raced across the field toward them. How would she stop the two from hurting her without breaking their bones or beating them unconscious? She needed to save Dad. *Find Aaron.* She could kill Lady Erica, that much she knew. These two reminded her too much of Dad and Josh.

Running uphill toward the parking lot and the black Ford, she left Sandy to follow. This wouldn't end well. If they chased her back up to the house with bruised ribs and bloody feet, she'd still have Lady Erica to deal with. *Where's Aaron?* If he truly came to help, wouldn't he be up at the house? Where had he been when they were chasing her? Or when they'd coerced Dad? *I can't count on him.* She had to find him, get Kiana's gun, and kill Lady Erica.

CHAPTER 34

Panting as she ran, Haddie searched the porch of the house at the top of the sloping upper vineyard. There was no sign of Lady Erica or her gun-wielding attendant. Sandy and the other coerced had dropped behind, even though they had shoes. The sun was setting close to the top of the western ridge, and breeze from the north brought the smell of storms. The gray asphalt rising beside the vineyard seemed steeper than the first time she'd walked it. The skin on the tops of Haddie's feet, between her toes, and around her ankles and shins still burned from using her powers, but the pads slapping on asphalt felt almost nothing.

Where would Aaron hide? She raced uphill, trying to imagine where she'd go when she reached the top. Sandy would catch her before she could hide. *I don't want to hide.* Kiana had been her only plan, and somehow, she'd broken her leg and given her weapon to Aaron. Hoping that Aaron might help seemed futile. *If I find him, I'll make him help.*

Somewhere to the left, the familiar song rang again. Wincing as she twisted her side, Haddie glanced back. It couldn't get any worse, and whoever had used their powers below hadn't been after her. Sandy had dropped even farther behind. A woman called out, close to the pool. *One of the models?* Haddie clenched her jaw and ignored it, keeping her eyes on the doors and windows of the house.

The doors to the house stood open. The table where they'd been eating was empty. No one moved inside. As impossible as it seemed, no one came out to challenge Haddie. The windows and doors on the corner looked in on a warmly lit bedroom. If they believed she'd been chased away, they may have relaxed their guard. Maybe Haddie could slip in, surprise Lady Erica, and make her vanish. Before Sandy caught up with her? Aaron and the gun were her best chance. *No, they're probably long gone.* Did Dad still lie on the lawn, twitching?

The open doors to the dining area seemed inviting, but where was everyone?

The flagpole rose on a mulched mound at the top of the vineyard; fragrant flowering bushes dotted the landscape between the white fence and the grass that circled the house. Sandy had disappeared. Hiking the remains of her dress higher, Haddie climbed over the fence to search the drive for her pursuers. Where had they gone?

Crouching, Haddie approached the porch. She could see some of the others, first by their yellow haze, and then by their shapes around the dining area. Chairs and plates had fallen to the floor. One woman lay on her side with her eyes closed as if sleeping. Another sat against the wall so that Haddie only saw extended legs, one with a bare foot, and glowing coercion through the wall. Like Dad, they didn't seem to be doing well under Lady Erica's effect. Had Josh gone through this?

Haddie almost imagined slipping through them; they didn't appear threatening. *I can't risk them calling out.*

Checking back for her missing pursuers, she crawled onto the porch.

On the far end, where Lady Erica would have been standing when she coerced Dad, a body lay. It could have been the man with a goatee who'd been shot. *Dead?* Had they left him to bleed out?

With still no sign of Sandy or her accomplice, Haddie stepped closer to the house.

The corner bedroom with the double doors was larger than the one she'd climbed out on the other side. Clothes were piled on this bed too. The lights were on, but no one moved inside. *Please, be unlocked.*

On one knee, Haddie opened the door Quietly, she stood and stepped in. She recognized one of the outfits, a purple dress. Both pairs of heeled shoes were too small and would not serve well if she had to run. A partial bloody footprint aimed toward her from near the bureau. *Strange.* She crossed the floor, leaving her own bloody trail.

She paused at the doorway to the hall. To her left, a door led to a bedroom with a fireplace. On the opposite wall, a glass-paned door could have led to a hall, or perhaps additional rooms. With her hand on the doorway, she shifted to catch a glimpse of a large stove and wood shelving. The smell of something dead hung in the air, mixed with the interrupted dinner. She'd have to pass the dining room. Haddie sighed and leaned forward to look down the hall into the rest of the house.

Lady Erica waited there, standing as regal as before in front of two heavy wooden doors. She offered a light smirk as Haddie started. *Is she waiting for me?* Her attendant with the tablet stood behind her, looking down as if preoccupied.

Haddie hummed in defense.

The blonde lover with wide eyes stood to the side,

backlit from the sunroom. Dad slumped on his knees in front of her.

"Don't dally," Lady Erica said. Her painted skin and pink hair made her stand out against the others.

Haddie could run out the way she'd come in. She'd left the door unlocked. *Am I ready to give up on Dad?*

They'd stripped his jacket and shirt off. A bloody bandage had been hastily wrapped around the gunshot wound in his arm; his skin had blood smeared from armpit to waist.

He knelt on the floor with his face slack, as if drunk. The young lover, yellow haze covering her eyes, pressed a large, serrated bread knife against his throat. Haddie could make the threat disappear. Lady Erica waited for her chance. Dark red lips smiled in a quiet smirk.

"You've ruined my party." Lady Erica snickered at her own comment. "You deserve to be punished." She flicked a gloved hand in the air and frowned, creasing her white painted face. "Cut his cheek, just a little bit."

The lover removed the knife from his neck and drew a red line across his cheek, as carefully as if she painted it there. Dad didn't resist.

"No." Haddie sucked in a breath, easing out toward the hall and holding onto the door frame.

The cook huddled on the floor at the edge of the kitchen, staring at his hands. She could see some of the others, scattered in various positions around the dining table.

"Kill her," Lady Erica said to Dad.

He blinked slowly. *Dad won't do it.* Haddie already had her protection humming, but could she fight off both of them? His lips moved, as if he mumbled something she couldn't hear. *Dad?*

Lady Erica sighed and frowned. "Sister? Daughter?" She could have been asking either one of them.

She doesn't have full control of him yet. Haddie took another step into the hall. Her heart pounded. If she attacked, the lover would have to be the first target. Could she attack all of them at once? Dad had done it, in her visions.

Sandy and the other coerced would be there soon, but in the meantime, Lady Erica was nearly unprotected. *I could force her to free Dad.* Her muscles tensed and she unconsciously widened her stance.

Lady Erica stepped to the side, behind the coerced lover and Dad. Her movement exposed the short, dark-haired man who had fired a gun earlier. He stepped forward, reloading it.

The bread knife hung to the side of Dad's face. He didn't seem to notice it, nor the blood that trickled down his cheek. The yellow haze clung to his eyes.

Lady Erica sang a high, clear note. Haddie's defenses held, though the force of it staggered her. Dad and the lover swayed.

The assistant finished loading the gun and lifted it. As bad a shot as he'd proven himself to be, he couldn't miss at that distance. She could make him disappear, but then she'd lose to Lady Erica.

Haddie screamed. She focused inward, pushing herself back in time as she had Kiana. *Just a nudge.* Dad had said that intent was everything.

PART 5

We can break their cycle of violence and destruction and bring peace to the peoples of Earth.

CHAPTER 35

In a blink, the room brightened and became empty of people, its chairs straightened. Pain sheared across her skin. Haddie staggered at the feeling of her flesh being split and torn away. She sucked in ragged breaths. The room smelled like lemon cleaning solution and still that taint of death.

She dropped to her knees in the hall, and the visions swept away the present. Dad used his power on a bear racing toward him. Haddie found herself standing on a small farm with neat rows of green plants carved out of the woods. An old Ford parked near a rust-red barn. The second scene turned to darkness, with bombs flashing red and orange around her. A man drove a bayonet into Dad's friend before he disappeared. The last came during the same war, perhaps World War I from the odd helmets. She could smell the filth and sweat. Mud covered everything.

Gasping from the pain, she stared at a brown tile. Glazed, it reflected some of the sunlight. Someone spoke in another room. Not the kitchen or dining room in front of her, but close. *I've got to hide.* She had moved through time. The sun shone through skylights, and the house felt warmer. On hands and knees, she turned and scrambled toward the bedroom, hoping they wouldn't hear her. It seemed like moments before, she'd entered to find Lady Erica. Her dress dragged to the side, threatening to catch under her knee. *What time is it? What day is it?* If she'd come back days earlier, wouldn't she have warned herself? *Unless I don't survive.*

She'd done this to Kiana, who had used the time to prepare for Barbara Stevens in Boise. *Maybe that's what I did — am going to do.* Carefully closing the door behind her, she found herself back in the bedroom with a large cream-colored bed and double doors. Three pairs of flip flops lined the floor in front of a bureau, and bikinis piled on top. She smeared the floor with a footprint as she moved to stand. Sitting, Haddie slid a pair of orange flip flops onto her swollen feet with shaking hands. The bottoms were as torn as she'd feared.

Candles and rock salt lights littered the surfaces, but there wasn't one clock. Kiana had found time to get a rifle and put a bullet in Barbara's skull. Haddie would be willing to do that if she had money, a car, and the time. Maybe they had weapons stashed here. What if it were weeks or months before the fashion show?

It feels like summer. There were people here, perhaps cleaning and cooking for the dinner. The bikinis had been laid out for the models. *It's today.*

I need a weapon. She idly reached for a bureau drawer. Empty. They wouldn't hide guns in the bedroom. The garage out back? In an office? The kitchen? With her hand on the bureau for support, she knelt and then rose to her feet. Her skin felt as raw as the bottom of her feet looked, bloody and torn. *Garage.*

The double doors opened to the vineyard. The two side windows looked at the flagpole and driveway to her right.

Haddie unlocked the doors and opened one slowly. No alarm rang. Closing it carefully behind her, she padded quietly across the wood and stepped off the porch onto manicured grass. The picket fence lay just on the other side of flowering bushes bedded in mulch. Still numb, her feet barely registered her movement, but at least she wasn't making them worse.

A white catering van was parked in the lot behind the house with its back doors open. It had backed in as if to unload at the double gate of the white picket fence.

Haddie crouched. She'd heard a voice, which meant at least one person worked inside, likely more. Trailing her black dress through shrubs and mulch, she stepped to the fence by the driveway. Leaning on the lamp atop a post, she climbed over. Her dress snagged on the pointed edge of a picket.

Behind the house, pans rattled and grew louder. Someone moved outside. *Damn.* Haddie dropped to the asphalt, and her dress ripped enough to hang on the fence, the white tip sticking through her black hem. Her side complained at the sudden pressure against the driveway. She peeked through the slats and watched a young man in a gray uniform carry a stack of metal pans to the open doors of the van. He slid them in and closed the doors. If he got in the van, he couldn't drive away without seeing her. Haddie winced, scuttling backward and frantically trying to loosen her dress enough to free it.

The worker pulled jingling keys from his pocket and headed for the driver's door. *I can't lie here.* Haddie yanked, and the dress ripped free. He must have heard, before pausing to glance back toward the house. A chill crawled up her shoulders despite the sun. The asphalt smelled like earth and tires. The man continued quickly to the van door and grabbed the handle.

Haddie lurched into a roll that flashed pain up her side. The unyielding asphalt found every bruise and scratch. Her skin still felt raw. The opposite side of the drive sloped into a swale where oak trees grew to cover the driveway in shade. Haddie rolled to the bottom in a blur. The van started, and she crawled to the nearest tree. *Not very hidden, Haddie.* She didn't dare crawl uphill into the brush.

Her chest tightened as the van's transmission thudded into gear. She held her breath, her yellow wig hidden against the tree trunk, as tires droned across the asphalt. Picking up speed, the man drove past and down the hill.

Haddie lay there, breathing in an out, and waited for her heart to calm. *I need to find out what time it is. I need a weapon.* In the near future, Dad would be coerced. If she altered that future, then she might not be back here to do something about it. What had Lady Erica done to Dad after she vanished? Would they kill him? *No.* They wanted him to join them, and coerced, he had no choice. Her fists curled tight. She remembered the cute little blonde lover holding that bread knife to his throat. No one would get in her way this time.

Rising slowly, Haddie crept toward the garage. It rose off the slope on a concrete foundation so that the front lay level with the back parking lot.

When she reached the corner of the garage, she could see the back of the house. The sidewalk cut through the grass to the corner that the two wings of the house created. This was the same path she'd originally taken with Dad. The doors were open, but no one moved within sight of the backyard or the windows.

Haddie stood and walked behind the garage. The windows were locked. The inside looked empty. She tapped out one of the panes with a stick and ran to the side to check the house. If anyone had heard, they didn't come out.

Unlocking the broken window, Haddie managed to cut a finger. Inside, she found little more than a hammer, a flimsy leaf rake, and a hand saw. Not what she imagined for her trouble. It seemed no one actually lived on the property, though Lady Erica had called it her getaway in the mountains.

Through the front windows of the garage door, she could see the house clearly. The kitchen looked over the backyard, and she could see at least one man working inside. He came to the sink for a moment but disappeared again. The doors through which she'd originally been led inside were open.

On the far side, where she and Dad had initially tried to escape, she'd imagined there would be more bedrooms, or maybe an office with a clock or even a weapon hidden in a desk. It seemed less likely after her search of the garage. The shadows on the porch looked like it could be just past midday. *I've got to take a chance.*

If she crossed the backyard, the man could easily see her. The kitchen had too many windows.

Haddie made her way out through the broken window and followed the swale down the drive toward the front of the house. The windows on the side looked into bedrooms. She knew from her previous visit that the kitchen and dining area took up the center. *I need to search the far side where Dad will be coerced.* She climbed the fence when she reached the vineyard and crouched between the rows. The dining room doors were open, and through them she spotted the cook moving in the kitchen.

The first room on the front corner with the most windows looked like a sunroom. Haddie made her way between the grape vines, watching for the cook or any movement. Once she passed the corner room, it seemed safe to approach the house. She crept onto the porch and tested the windows as she peered into the bedrooms. Bathing suits had been laid out in preparation for the models. The room they'd escaped from looked different without the piles of discarded fashion show outfits. Haddie turned to the lawn where Dad would be coerced, then to the stairs, and finally the chapel. If she had a gun, she could wait in the chapel and kill Lady Erica before any of it ever started. Then none of it would happen. She shook her head. *I need a plan through the complete loop, like Kiana did.* I can't risk what might happen to myself if I don't have a reason to disappear back in time.

At the end of the house inside the last locked window, she found an office. Little more than a desk and a couple chairs furnished the room. Haddie froze. High above the desk, a cordless phone sat in a small black cradle on a shelf with a router of some sort. The porch creaked as she hurried around a corner to the door at the back of the room. A white trash bag, hardly full, sat on the porch beside a grill.

Please, please. Breaking the window did not seem like a good option. Haddie tried the knob, and it turned. Almost hurrying with excitement, she opened the door and slipped inside. *I should look for weapons, too.* This would be the room. She went straight for the phone.

The display on the phone showed 2:11, and she confirmed the date. Haddie held it and stared at the keypad. Dad had made her memorize his and Kiana's numbers, but she questioned what she imagined she remembered.

The line hissed with static but gave her a dial tone.

Haddie dialed Dad. He'd be in the hotel, maybe not even getting phone service. He'd get the message. He hadn't. *Maybe this time he will.* If she saved him, would she disappear? Some time warp thing? *I should have called Terry first. He'd know.*

It jumped to voicemail. No greeting from Dad. Someone's voicemail. *He hadn't set it up.* She had to hope it was his. Her voice quiet, she spoke with her hand cupped around the phone and her mouth. "Dad. Don't let us get on the bus. Make me act like I'm sick." Haddie swallowed. *This isn't going to work.* "Lady Erica is going to coerce you."

It wouldn't work. It hadn't. Very likely it had been the wrong number. She pressed the end call button.

Less confident, she dialed Kiana. The static grew loud as it rang. *I probably have both numbers mixed.* She pulled the phone away as she heard footsteps inside the house.

Someone picked up on the other end of the line. "Kiana?" Haddie asked in cupped whisper.

The footsteps stopped.

"Haddie?" Kiana asked.

Haddie flushed with relief and spat out her sentences in hushed snippets. "Dad's been coerced. Will be. They caught us. I need your help."

A voice called from within the house with a slightly nasal accent. "Hello?" *The cook?*

Someone had heard. Cringing, Haddie almost hung up. "Bring Aaron."

Kiana spoke too loudly. "Wait, what? *What* about Thomas?"

"Hello?" the man called out again. Haddie hung up. Grimacing, she tried to put the phone in its base silently. She could come back to it later. The back door still ajar, she slipped out and closed it carefully. The porch creaked lightly underfoot.

"Hello?" The voice sounded in the office she'd just left.

She froze, leaning against the corner, just two thin strips of wall between the door and window; she'd be seen from either.

CHAPTER 36

"Lady Erica?"

She stood stiffly, examining the useless recruits on the floor. The wind had picked up, blustering the scent of the coming storm into the house, a welcome change to whatever rotted. *This house has too many windows.* She'd never felt so exposed or threatened, at least not for a long time. Her New York penthouse felt safe. It would again, when she got out of this mess.

Tyrone held out the tablet. The General's message read, "Reinforcements on the way. ETA 6:15 p.m. Urgent that you retain control of target at any cost."

She checked the time on the tablet: 4:53 p.m. The woman had disappeared, even as Tyrone put a bullet through her. *Where had she gone?* Lady Erica looked at the man kneeling on the floor with his wound. *What power did she have — they have?*

Carolyn would be arriving before the General's reinforcements. Where were Dylan's monstrosities? One had been in the vineyards. Had the woman or the man made them disappear? *Where did they go?* Most important, would they be back? She feared Dylan's creatures as much as this other woman with powers. There had been that other song as well. A third companion of the man and the woman?

Do I wait here or try to leave? She had people to work with, but only the blonde, large-eyed woman had responded quickly. "Protect me," she called to her pets.

The man kneeling at her feet, the target the General cherished, roused and stood swaying. She would no doubt link him to the General after they escaped. Her more important targets were quickly transferred to his control. It didn't matter; she had no use for them.

One of the women on the far side of the dining table pulled a chair to the floor with her attempt to stand. Another with straight black hair managed to actually stand and stumbled toward them for a step before crashing to the floor. *What do I lack, that my ancestors mastered?* Her visions had revealed nearly instant obedience. These would recover enough in the next day or two.

Looking carefully at the doe-eyed woman, she said, "Go outside." She pointed to the back. "Start the car." The guards had likely kept the keys on them, but there might be a chance. The woman stumbled, but made her way toward the corridor leading out the back, carrying her bread knife. Early on, commands had to be handled literally and in simple steps.

Her body ached. She stood at the center of the house with walls, or at least heavy doors, at her back and where she could exit through any of the other directions from her position. Still, she could hardly feel safe. Someone had slipped too close. There would be no more recruiting parties. Sandy and Carolyn could handle all that. If Sandy survived.

Tyrone stood quietly at her shoulder.

"Did you reload the gun?" she asked.

"No, Mistress." He stood there. "Shall I?"

She nodded, and he headed through the heavy wooden doors to the office in the back.

The General will know if I leave. As long as she brought his man, it shouldn't matter. He hadn't specified that she wait in the house. Even if the car didn't start, she would leave when Carolyn arrived. She had never wanted to be a part of his plan. No matter how many times she'd contemplated suicide, and tried, the thought of dying terrified her. *One way or another, I'm leaving.*

CHAPTER 37

HADDIE HELD HER BREATH. Three hesitant footsteps sounded from the office, then silence.

The birds and insects created a cacophony of sounds from the woods and the tree just in front of her. The grass had an earthy smell. She closed her eyes, drowning it all out and focusing on the man's movement inside. *What happens if he opens that door?* If she ran away, it would have been reported to Lady Erica that someone had been snooping on the property. That hadn't seemed to have happened. *Over two hours from now.*

Another footstep brought the man to the door. She thought of shifting farther around the corner of the porch, but she'd expose herself in the window. The stairs that she took earlier — later — were across the lawn. Surely the boards would creak if she adjusted her position. She'd move if he turned the knob, but if he pressed against the door to look out, he would surely see her.

The handle beside her spun in a quick click, but the door didn't open. She held her breath. *I can tell him I work for Lady Erica.* Inspecting the grounds for the party. In a torn black dress, orange flip flops, and a blonde wig hanging on with pins?

The lock clicked on the door. Footsteps retreated.

Haddie sucked in a breath of air, then let it out slowly to calm herself. *I need a plan.* She'd searched the garage and as much of the house as she dared. The cook obviously could hear her inside the house. In a couple hours, Kiana would bring the only weapon Haddie could count on, but it hadn't worked out that way. Somehow Kiana had gotten hurt, and Aaron had the gun.

She viewed the lawn where Dad would be coerced. Lady Erica would be standing on the opposite end of the porch, near the front. The chapel would have been the best place to shoot from. That had never happened, though. If Haddie had gotten to Kiana in time they would have killed Lady Erica when she first stepped out of the dining area onto the front porch, before she coerced Dad.

I have to build my plan for when I move myself back in time. It would start when Kiana and Aaron arrived. They had likely parked somewhere along the road. Haddie had never seen anything of the road while trapped inside the party bus with the shades pulled and colorful lights. She didn't remember much of the ride. It had been terrifying to have the two demons only a few footsteps away.

She would have to guess where Kiana would stop following the bus; Haddie could wait there for her. That meant a long walk with shredded feet and aching ribs. She had time to search the chapel and the pool area first. They might have phones, or something she could use. *Going back in the house isn't an option.* What point was there to searching any other buildings? This appeared to be an empty vacation house.

So, what's my plan? Haddie peeked in the window. The

cook did not stand there waiting. The room was clear, and the phone sat on the shelf. *Who am I going to call anyway?* In truth, she'd die for a quick call to Liz or Sam. They always helped put things in perspective, even if she couldn't tell Sam the details.

Haddie swallowed and stepped onto the grass. If Haddie couldn't free Dad, Sam and Meg were in danger. *Is that the way it works, or do they just do what they're told?* Would he expose them all?

She watched the windows as she walked in case the cook lingered in a different room. Everything in her life would change, and in her friends' lives. Terry already had the FBI breathing down his neck. Dad's coercion could only make that worse. She couldn't go near David, for fear of involving him.

Crouching as she passed the sunroom's expansive set of windows, Haddie could see the dining room tables. In a few hours, she'd be sitting there with Dad. *I can't lose Dad. I don't want to be alone.*

The grass on the side of the vineyard led to where she would break the fence when she would tumble through. The slope she'd fallen down appeared less steep than when she'd been rolling. Still, it didn't look like something anyone would climb up. Everything seemed impossible at the moment.

I need to rest. Exhausted, she sat on the grass. She had time before Kiana would arrive. Her dress hung useless to the side, and she re-knotted it. Blood stained the orange flip flops. Scratches covered her legs and arms. Her hands were dotted with purpura. She put her forehead to her knees, and winced at the contact. Blonde hair scratched at the side of her face.

I'm not losing Dad.

Haddie tore at her wig; it dangled lopsided anyway. Ignoring the pain as hairs pulled out of her tender scalp, she yanked pins. *I need to free Dad. I need a weapon.* Kiana had brought one. *I need that gun.* She tossed the wig into the brush where she'd fallen — where she would fall.

CHAPTER 38

AARON TAPPED the armrest while he watched the road ahead. The SUV acceleration forced him back in his chair as Kiana passed a work truck with bouncing ladders strapped out the back. They had lost sight of the bus and the car that trailed it. He had seen the glow of the two inside earlier and had no desire to get too close. *Why am I doing this?*

The country road wove upward into the mountains, and he had given up on getting any signal on his phone. It would last a couple minutes and then disappear. Towns came and went, or at least clusters of buildings. *Where are they going?* It did not seem like the road could keep on without crossing over the mountains.

He should not have gotten in the car. Thomas put himself in his position. Kiana had her own reasons to race off and try to rescue him. *What is my excuse?*

Haddie had said that Thomas had been coerced. They had lost. Everything would be over. Terry had no chance. *I should warn him.* Still, he sat driving toward another Boise. He had refused. Then, somewhere in the middle of the argument, he had agreed to stay with the car while Kiana scouted the grounds. That had been over an hour ago, and he had been regretting the decision every minute since.

"Where could they be going?" Kiana sounded frustrated.

He swallowed as he saw the taillights of the guard's car. "This could all be a trap." The bus showed for a moment, then disappeared between the trees and a curve.

"I'm not leaving Thomas. We'll figure something out." Kiana's jaw clenched.

He had seen her upset before. *This is different.* She had grown close to Thomas, perhaps too close. It would put them at risk if she did not think rationally.

Would he stay in the car? *Not likely.* Haddie and Thomas had gotten through scrapes before. If he could offer some help, he would. If Kiana kept rational.

"What do you plan to do?" he asked.

She tugged on her ear. "I won't know that until I see the situation. I'll scout out the perimeter and see what my options are."

It sounded reasonable, but so had Boise. He couldn't tell her about the demons on the bus. It would mean exposing his own abilities, if she didn't already know. "We need to be careful. There could be demons guarding Lady Erica as well." A traffic light early on had forced them near the bus, where he'd barely seen two glowing orange pinpoints.

"Considering the escorts, it's possible."

He'd seen her pack a gun. *I should have checked if Thomas brought one.* The man wouldn't have gone to the fashion show with it, but he hardly needed a weapon. He was one.

"I'll help you scout, if I can carry the gun.'

Kiana's lips pursed. "We'll see."

"If you decide to jump in and rescue him, I'll give it back and wait in the car." Likely, he'd hide and watch the car.

She nodded, but didn't say anything.

The road climbed on, and his chest grew tighter. This group that had coerced Thomas had larger plans. At some point, someone would have to try and stop them. Haddie and the others had already started by killing Sameedha and Barbara Stevens. *I want to help.* He just couldn't risk using his abilities.

CHAPTER 39

HADDIE'S LEGS ached as she walked down the drive. Her skin chafed wherever her clothes touched. The rhythm of her flip flops on the asphalt kept her going. *Where would Kiana park?*

The birds called out from the woods on each side of the road. A feeble breeze brought an earthy smell from the north. *No scent of rain yet.* That would come later. She'd passed the point where she'd found Kiana the first time. *Maybe an hour from now?* She paused and searched the trees and brush on each side, then back uphill toward the house. The curve let the woods obscure it, but she imagined she would still be able to see the bus from here. *A little farther.*

Lady Erica would arrive soon, give her speech, and walk everyone up to the house. Two guards and two demons would wait near the bus. The other two coerced would park up by the garage, and later die in the bedroom from which she and Dad would escape. *I need to get Kiara's gun.* She'd shoot the lover who had cut Dad and the attendant with the tablet. Perhaps she'd even put a bullet in Lady Erica's leg, just so she'd be motivated to release Dad. If possible, they'd drag the woman back to Eugene and have her fix Josh. *Nothing will get in my way this time.*

Ahead along the right side of the road, a field stretched out where the woods ended. Haddie turned uphill where the pavement curved. She was probably being overly cautious, but she could follow the bus after the escorts passed. She stepped off the road where the woods had a drier smell than the wind. Up at the house, the last time, she hadn't noticed the scent of the approaching storm, but now it hung in the breeze.

Among the trees and low grass, she found a shrub and crouched beside it. *Too exposed.* A little deeper in, she found a rotting fallen tree. At a thicker section where a knot and limb reached up, she climbed behind and lay down to gauge how much it hid her white hair and black dress. The driver would be the only one with visibility from the bus. The blinds had all been pulled. The coerced guards in the escort vehicles would likely be focused on the road, not the woods. *I hope.* Already she'd climbed pretty deep into the woods. The slope had begun to drop away sharply, so any farther, the incline would hide the traffic.

The air seemed to cool even as she lay there. The numbness had begun to fade in her feet, unfortunately, so every cut and scrape felt swollen and damp. A pair of gnats harassed her at one point, and she grimaced angrily as she sat and swatted at them. *Focus, Haddie.*

What if she couldn't save Dad? Everyone would be in danger. Liz, Meg, Sam, and Terry would have to run. Perhaps the person who wrote the letter, the person who must be behind all this, not care about them now that Lady

Erica had Dad coerced? They'd been looking for Harold Holmes, and with Dad they'd know exactly where he was. A smear in his basement.

Maybe Kiana had heard and understood Haddie's call. She and Aaron might have at least warned Terry, who could get hold of Liz. Sam, Meg, and Rock would never know. *Meg.* If the people who had hunted her before were the same people, they'd go after her. Dad would do anything to stop that. *He'd want me to stop it.*

Haddie's chest felt suddenly empty. She couldn't hurt Dad. *Not even for Sam, Rock, or Meg.* Her throat swelled thick, and she fought tears. Rolling onto her back, she stared up at the fuzzy canopy of leaves filtering the blue sky. *I can't.* She shouldn't have agreed to go to the dinner, but she'd wanted to see Lady Erica after driving all the way down to San Francisco. *Selfish.* Tears flowed as she imagined Sam's face and Dad's. The birds nearby quieted as she sobbed.

The sound of the bus passing jerked her into a sitting position, then the sight of the coerced guards driving behind it dropped her back down. Rubbing tears from her eyes, she rolled over and watched as they sped uphill. "Damn." Haddie tried to jump up, tore her dress a little more, and tumbled back onto her knees until she could get it out from under her feet.

The climb back up to the road took too long. Her RAV4 crawled past. "Wait. Kiana!" Haddie yelled. Her car disappeared around the corner. *Surely Kiana won't get too close.* Uphill in flip flops with feet that cringed at each step didn't help her make it to the road quickly.

Swearing, Haddie scrambled up to the side of the road and jogged cautiously along the asphalt. Kiana had gone much farther than expected. The trip downhill had gone quickly, mindlessly. *What was I thinking?*

Her legs ached and joints still burned from using her power. Now the pavement seemed to curve through an endless forest that gave no hint of the house or vineyards high above. Even the mountains and ridges were hidden by the trees. Sweat stuck her hair to her neck. *I should have waited closer.*

The RAV4 was parked ahead, on the ridge side of the road. Haddie crossed the pavement. The top of the bus showed between the trees. *Kiana parked awfully close.* Maybe she had heard about Dad and panicked. The nose of the SUV had been pulled into a thicket of light brush at the base of an oak. Still, if the guards walked to the edge of the parking lot, they would likely be able to see it. If they looked.

Kiana should see me by now. Haddie slowed as she approached the back of the RAV4. In the shade, she couldn't see inside or a face in the side mirror. They weren't there.

They're searching for me. Haddie looked into the back, cupping her hands against the tint. She hadn't seen them on the road. How long had it taken for her to run to the car? *Too long.* Where had they gone? Feeling nauseous, she swallowed and stared uphill. *Where would I go if I were them?* Kiana might be upset and trying to get to the bus or the house. From the message and the timing, she might not realize that Dad hadn't been coerced yet. *Now is all that matters.*

Crouching, Haddie jogged along the side of the road toward the spot where she'd found Kiana with a broken leg. On the other side of the road, the woods thinned, giving way to the lower vineyard before climbing up to the parking lot. There was more cover on the west side of the house where the oaks grew thick on the slope of the ridge. Time was running out. In a few minutes, they'd be discovered at the house and begin their escape — her escape, Dad's coercion.

As she feared, Kiana didn't lie in the same spot as she had before — later. Haddie continued past and trudged carefully uphill toward the corner of the vineyard where she would tumble through. A coerced guard stepped into view at the edge of the parking lot, and Haddie dashed behind a tree. The back of the bus stood out clearly, and the top of the SUV showed over the ridge of asphalt. From where she hid, the drive led up to the parking lot.

The man looked down at the vineyards from atop a sharp incline. He drew his gun, and Haddie searched the rows of grapes. Between the vines, she caught a glimpse of dangling yellow and orange. *Kiana's beads.* The man had spotted them. Did they know? Kiana moved toward Haddie. The guard had a clear shot. If nothing else, the gunshot would alert the demons.

Haddie growled. Her song rang and the guard faded.

She moaned at the pain that raged across her skin. It seemed to get worse each time. Holding onto the rough bark, she fell into the visions, horrific trenches and fields of death from the war. She slipped from one to the next, sickened at the gore and stench of death. *How had Dad endured these wars?* Just the nightmares of it made her want to give up on mankind.

During the episode, Haddie dropped to a knee beside the tree with her hand burning against the bark. She had to be prepared. The second guard could be on his way. *I can't move.* A stray lock of white hair dangled over her eye. Kiana paused to peer between plants directly at Haddie. Aaron shifted farther behind. *They saw me.* They must have been sneaking around the guards.

Trembling, Haddie tried to stand. Her feet burned and her knees buckled. She cried out when her palm grabbed the rough trunk. Kneeling beside the tree, she took deep breaths. *I need to get up.*

With eyelids thick and barely able to stay open, Haddie looked up at a motion near the parking lot. The second guard had arrived. He spotted Kiana easily and reached to his side as if for his weapon. Kiana dove to the ground, but the vineyard didn't offer any cover.

"Hell," Haddie murmured.

Anticipating the pain, she forced the growl. It seemed as if her body resisted, but she pushed it out. Her tone rang in the air around her, vibrating through her.

As he faded into mist, she hit the ground. A stalk of grass poked against her neck, spiking the pain worse than anywhere else, as if a great gash had ripped open. The sky sparkled with lights before the visions hit. She whimpered through the nightmares. Her eyes pressed shut, but the images, smells, and sounds of war consumed her. *Dad lived this.*

The scent of fresh earth and the coming storm welcomed her back to the present. She couldn't lift her head. Her eyes adjusted to light, showing the grass and weeds at her nose. A black edge hung at edges of her sight. Flesh tormenting her, she almost embraced unconsciousness.

Dad. Through most of college, she'd distanced from Dad. He'd kept secrets about his age and more. Now she knew them, and it had brought them closer again, close enough that she'd relied on his help this year. Then Meg happened, and Boise, yanking him out of her life. *I made that choice.* She could have joined them and lived quietly on the farm.

I pushed David away, too. Her throat swelled and tears threatened.

Uphill a gunshot sounded, and she started. Before the echo died in the trees, Dad's song rang out. By the house, Dad had been shot. *It's all happening again.*

Somewhere closer, a man called out and then started yelling frantically. Tilting her head, she turned toward the parking lot. The bus driver?

In just a couple minutes, Dad would be coerced.

I need to get to Dad. Haddie dragged a hand closer to her face, shifting her body. Her song rang out from above as her former self killed one of the coerced security guards. A gunshot joined her tone with a truncated snap.

The bus started, grinding gears.

One of the demons would be thrashing through the upper vineyard. Did it react to the gunshot or the song? Could they hear the tones? Where was the second demon?

Move, Haddie. If Haddie couldn't fix Dad, then she couldn't go back to David. She'd be on the run. All her friends would be at risk. Pushing her head up from the ground, she saw the bus backing up in the parking lot. Kiana crept toward her, crouched among the rows. Aaron hung farther back. The bus ground gears and started down the drive.

Dad's song rang out, and Haddie sucked in a breath. *I need to get up.*

From over by the pool, someone screamed, then another. Perhaps the second demon had gone after the models.

Kiana increased her stride, racing toward Haddie. The bus had started downhill, but she didn't stop. For a moment, it seemed that she might be in the bus's path. She ran quickly, reaching Haddie's side of the road before the bus picked up speed on the pavement.

A demon rode the top of the bus; strips of the roof had been torn up, and a piece hung in its jaws. Gruesome, it looked up from its metal prey with a flattened head of dark red flesh and horns that stuck out sidewise like a bull's. Glowing orange eyes burned bright above a muzzle filled with irregular teeth. It didn't notice Haddie in the grass, but focused on Kiana.

The bus veered across the road, nearly heading into the forest, then turned back sharply. The driver likely had heard the creature digging through the roof, trying to get at him.

The demon leapt, more like a dog than a human. Its perch swerved as it launched, legs sprawled ungainly and unsteady in the air. The creature rolled sideways and spun backward. For a brief moment, it looked helpless. Thick paws flailing, its hindquarters crashed into Kiana.

She flew into the brush upon impact.

The demon bounced. Skidding on the asphalt with sharp claws, it came to a crouching stop. Its head and orange eyes swayed slowly to focus on Kiana. Its medallion glowed a soft yellow.

Kiana didn't move. As if lifeless, she sprawled in the grass.

On the far side of the lot, out of sight. The models were yelling.

Turning its head, the demon looked first toward the sound, then sharply into the lower vineyard. It dashed off with a snarl, away from Kiana. *Toward Aaron?*

Haddie pushed up, working a foot under herself so she could stand. She would have had to use her powers if the demon had gone after Kiana. *I don't know if I can survive another.* Her body felt close to giving out. She couldn't be sure she hadn't passed out during the last visions.

Lady Erica's high note rung in the air.

Haddie's heart froze. *Dad.*

CHAPTER 40

Haddie's legs ached as she forced herself to both feet. The light touch of the ragged dress burned her skin on her left side. The straps of her flip flops cut into her flesh like razors. The bra felt like a rope tied tightly across her chest.

Gunshots sounded from the house. The bus wound out of sight down the road ahead, and the demon bounded through the lower vineyard, crashing through vines and stakes.

Kiana didn't move; she stretched out in the brush close to where she'd been before. *She's okay, this is before.* Haddie stumbled, trying to get her feet and joints to work properly. They rebelled against movement. *I can't take much more.* Her mind moved in steps as sluggish as her feet. The gunshots above stopped as she staggered in the grass.

"Aaron," Kiana raised a hand, pointing toward the lower vineyard. "That demon will kill him."

Haddie paused, watching the leaping red-fleshed creature. "You brought your gun?" *Aaron has it. She said so before.*

"Aaron has it." Kiana's voice weakened. "Thomas?"

"Coerced. I'm going to kill Lady Erica. I can only hope Liz is right." She had a chance if she saved Aaron and got the gun. "Wait here." She turned from Kiana and took a raspy breath.

Stumbling at first, Haddie forced herself to jog across the road. The slope from the parking lot angled sharply to the lower vineyard, which then graded slowly downhill. At the end of the rows there was bright green grass. The pool area?

The demon bounded in that direction. He was faster than she could move, but Aaron seemed to be gaining a lead on both of them. Her best course would be to follow the demon's trail and use her powers again. She could smell the creature; a foul taint of rancid blood hung in the air.

One way or another, she'd get the gun from Aaron and kill Lady Erica before she left. Why did Aaron have the gun? Why didn't he just kill the demon? She imagined herself turning and firing at the creature as it bounded toward her. *He's afraid.* Haddie didn't have the energy to be afraid anymore. Even her anger barely bubbled under the surface. She'd kill Lady Erica and anyone who got in her way. It wasn't their fault. She needed her dad and friends safe. Nothing else mattered anymore.

The demon flopped against the rows ahead, less gracefully than others she had seen. Her own footsteps scuffed the fresh earth. The vines whipped against tender skin, but she didn't flinch. At this point, she planned on going through anything, or anyone, that got in her way.

CHAPTER 41

Aaron raced through the end of the row of grapes and turned right toward the pool and its buildings. The screaming there had stopped, but he heard their voices. Tossed towels littered the area. Two young women in bathing suits crouched next to tables and chairs under one of the gazebos. They startled, watching him. The air smelled of chlorine. He jumped to the brick pavers and raced directly toward the women. The models reacted slowly. The demon snarled close behind, and screams broke out around the pool from the surrounding woods. *Would they be enough distraction?*

Why had it chased him? *Haddie and Kiana were right there.* The demons seemed almost mindless once they pursued. He counted on it.

The building had an open side to the left where the tables sat in the shade, and a closed section that likely housed a shower and toilet. He aimed straight for the arch between. *I just need a little space to draw the gun.* The demon moved fast and erratic, leaping instead of running. Its nails scraped close behind on the brick pavers. If he stopped to fire, it would be on him before he pulled the trigger.

The women scrambled over the chairs as he raced past.

The hill dropped off behind the open end of the building, and he nearly lost his step turning at the corner. The tables and chairs crashed, and the screams turned hysterical. Aaron took no time to look behind as he pounded uphill. Above, a white picket fence lined the edge of the parking lot. The demon might find the prey by the pool more enticing than Aaron scrambling up the steep incline. *If not, I made a poor choice.* From the screams and snarls, the creature remained below.

The hill leveled, and Aaron dug in his pocket for the gun. He faltered when he saw a movement between the white pickets.

Across the parking lot, at the bottom of the upper vineyard, Haddie climbed through the fence and began running back toward Kiana. The timing seemed wrong. He had left her with Kiana; how had she gotten closer to the house — and wearing the yellow wig?

Freeing the gun, he turned and crouched, searching for the demon. It hopped on the far side of the pool. Aaron aimed, but it would have been a wasted shot. Almost gleefully, the creature chased a model down a slope.

Haddie jogged behind, appearing almost drunk from her gait. *A second Haddie.*

Aaron turned back to the first Haddie, the one heading for Kiana. There, someone chased that Haddie from the edge of the forest beside the upper vineyard. *Standing here exposed. Idiot.* A large tree stretched over the white picket fence and the drive that led up to the house. He jogged to get in its shade and hide in the shadow. He lost sight of both Haddies. At the porch of the house, a tall woman with pink hair watched where Haddie ran toward Kiana. *Lady Erica, I presume.* Her photos had often shown her with bright hair.

Haddie had moved Kiana back in time in Boise. Had she done the same with herself? If so, her plan seemed to be going poorly. More likely, she had no plan. His best option would be to keep away from both of them. He had agreed to accompany Kiana if he carried the gun. Obviously necessary, considering how badly the situation had turned out.

I have no intention of dying over this. He had agreed to help Kiana, partially from curiosity, and partly from the guilt he felt over Haddie's coworker. She did not deserve to lose her father over this. Not that he believed he could help. Or would, if it meant using his power. Shooting the woman in the colorful wig, he could do, if it freed Thomas.

For now, he wanted to get farther away from the demon. Haddie could handle it better than he could.

A swale led to an outbuilding beside the house. The drive led up there, and one of the escorting SUVs had parked at the top. Perhaps a garage? It looked like a quiet place where he might be able to watch the house.

The demon chased the woman toward his hiding place under the tree. The incline was too steep.

Then again, no reason to chance it. Aaron quietly crouched beside the driveway and headed uphill.

CHAPTER 42

Haddie's legs weren't working properly as she ran. Her hip joints burned, and her knees seemed to give out at moments.

Except for muffled rustling in the woods, the leaping demon, and a screaming model, the area seemed silent; even the wind and birds kept quiet. Behind the pool's pavilions, the demon disappeared over a ridge, likely chasing Aaron into the wooded ravine. A model bled on the poolside, red gashes across her chest. There was no time to check on her. *Not likely she'll survive.*

Any other models had stopped their screaming, and only the occasional noise in the woods gave any indication they were still present, or alive. The only signs of them were the abandoned towels strewn about.

Haddie ran onto the brick pool deck, following the demon and hopefully Aaron. *I'll have to use my power.* She needed the gun, at any cost. Lady Erica would still be up at the house, and Haddie's former self would be facing her soon. When she returned, the odds would not have changed unless she had a weapon. *I have the element of surprise.*

With Dad held hostage, and a possible threat, she needed more than a covert attack.

The edge of the deck dropped into a thick forest. Easing down the back side of the pool, she caught sight of brush moving in the steep valley. The slope descended quickly from where she stood and more gently toward the back. Haddie moved along the edge of the pool area, searching for any signs of the demon or Aaron. Her previous fall kept her steps cautious.

The leaping lurch of red flesh farther to the south quickened Haddie's pace toward the back. A bikini-clad woman raced between oak trunks, and the demon hopped after her. She escaped toward the incline leading back toward the house, then scrambled in leaves and brush, her route turned toward Haddie and the easier slope up to the pool.

Where is Aaron? Considering the dying woman at the pool, he might already be dead. A chill rose up Haddie's neck. *I'd been angry, but I don't want him dead.* He'd come with Kiana, after all. The brush along the hill could hide a body. Had the demon followed Aaron there and gone after the model instead? *After it killed him?*

Haddie paused. She couldn't even be sure Aaron had come this way. The last she'd seen of him, he'd been running down the row of grapes. Searching the area north and east around the pool, she turned back to the more likely woods around the demon.

The woman, cheeks flushed pink and scratches across her legs, spotted Haddie and turned her mad scrabbling up the hill toward her. "Help!"

Aaron or not, leaving this thing running havoc wouldn't work if she intended to face Lady Erica.

As the demon leaped in the air above the model,

Haddie's song came out with a whine. The beast faded in red mist that trailed back down to the brush.

The pain across her skin dug into her flesh. Her legs gave out, and she slammed onto rough grass. Sliding feet first down the hill, the visions turned her world black.

Nightmares swirled around her. They dragged her into the hell of blood, war, and mud. She drifted endlessly into them, appearing to repeat and expand on each scenario.

When she woke, dirt and grass hung at the lips of her drooling mouth. Her dress was bundled up under her chin, and her body burned. Brush wedged between her legs and arms, and sunlight filtered through leaves hanging from a branch overhead. *Still daylight.*

Her power had never hit her like that before. Haddie trembled as she pushed up. How long had she been unconscious? The model was nowhere to be seen. The tops of the pavilions at the edge of the pool seemed impossibly far up the incline. Pain pulsed along her skin. Her thighs and stomach had new scrapes and grass stains Kneeling to adjust her bra, she smoothed down what was left of her dress. Lights speckled her vision.

She'd lost a sandal in the tumble and tenderly took a step to look around behind her. Aaron did not lay mangled among the leaves. Her pace had been slower than the demon, but there hadn't been enough time for it to chase down and kill Aaron, then begin hunting the model. If so, Aaron's body would have been close.

How late is it? Haddie tried to judge the sun's position on the western ridge. The northern storm had crept to the edge of the horizon, leaving a gray haze on the hills there. She could smell it on the wind. *What if Lady Erica had left already?*

She needed the gun. "Aaron?" If he hid nearby, he didn't respond. No one replied from the silence.

She plodded toward the higher ridge where the drive curved along the white picket fence. *I've got to get to her, weapon or not. The hammer?*

Above, Sandy climbed over the white picket fence, kitchen knife in hand.

Haddie tensed, taking a deep breath. *I'm in no shape for a fight.* If she wanted to get up to the house, she'd have to deal with the coerced woman. Imagining the cut on her dad's cheek, she clenched her jaw. Her feet still hurt, the bare one especially, but she stomped toward Sandy. The slope rose steeply, leveled out, and then angled up to the fence that bordered the drive.

Sandy showed no fear or reservation running down to the level ridge just above Haddie. Her pleasant affect gone and yellow haze glowing, she grimaced in determination. Hesitating only enough to turn sideways, she climbed downhill with the knife extended.

For the first time, Haddie wanted to hurt her. Too much had happened. *I'm too exhausted.* This coerced woman came between her and Dad. Gritting her teeth, Haddie lunged forward, dropping a knee to brace herself. She grabbed the woman's foot and pulled her off-balance.

Sandy thrust at the same moment. The blade tip jabbed a hand's width from Haddie's eye.

Damn. Haddie moved too slowly, but Sandy had already buckled and lost footing. The knife veered as the woman fell, and Haddie barely managed to flick her arm aside. As Sandy slid past, she slashed wildly with the blade.

Haddie lurched back and hit the grass. Her bare foot dug into the turf as she slid.

Sandy adjusted badly, nearly standing, before

momentum toppled her. Grunting, she landed on her side, bounced, and rolled down the slope. The metal knife glinted as it flew on its own path. She crashed toward the brush at the bottom where Haddie had awakened earlier.

Clinging onto tufts of grass and driving her nails into the dirt, Haddie managed to avoid sliding down with the coerced woman. Hugging the slope, it almost felt comfortable, like a momentary respite. *Get up, Haddie! Dad.* She braced and looked back, searching downhill.

Sandy lay nestled in the brush against a tree, alive, but certainly unconscious. The yellow haze still clung to her face.

Haddie felt no satisfaction or enjoyment from hurting the woman. Exhausted, she felt little emotion at all. Digging her feet into the grass, Haddie knelt, rose, and carefully continued her climb. *Sandy will survive, I imagine.* If Haddie could stop Lady Erica, then the woman might even be free.

Without bothering to climb over the fence, Haddie walked up the shallow swale lined with oaks toward the garage. Lady Erica's song rang out, and Haddie crouched. The note fell flat. Haddie searched the porch of the house, unable to see clearly inside. In a moment, the tone of her own song rang and filled the air. *I've pushed myself back in time.* The circle was complete.

Lady Erica wouldn't kill Dad. She'd try to leave, surely. Rushing, Haddie jogged through leaves toward the garage and a hammer. *A gun would be better.* Where is Aaron? He very well could be hiding down in that valley behind the pool. Or beating it back toward the RAV4. Hopefully Kiana had the keys and wouldn't let him take it.

Haddie turned at a noise too close behind her.

The coerced man who had been collecting invitations

thrashed noisily through the leaves as he raced up behind her. *I forgot about him.* She stopped, her hands clenched at her sides. *I don't have time for this.* She had never made a plan for Lady Erica, and now they'd completed the time loop. *I've wasted my chance.* She loosened her fingers and took a breath.

The man's knife gone, he lunged at her with both hands. The yellow haze obscured his wide eyes, but his jaw clenched tightly.

Haddie reacted without thinking. She leaned toward him while shifting her back foot to the side. Her punch caught him in the throat. Too low, but it snapped his head back. The top half of his body twisted in the air, and she kept clear of his arms. His feet tangled. When he landed, his head slammed against the roots of an oak. Even as he hit, his body skidded and rolled. Blood wet his hair, but the haze did not vanish. He still lived.

Haddie panted, her nerves tense. The joints of her fingers ached from the impact even though she'd hit no bones. "Stay," she said, as if he were an errant dog. Sagging, she thought of Rock as she continued toward the garage. Sam and Meg would hardly be worrying yet. They might wonder later tonight, if they didn't get a call from Dad. *I need to save him.* How could she force Lady Erica? First, get rid of her guards.

Stepping carefully around the man, she pulled on the tree trunk for support and hurried uphill. The wind carried the scent of the storm. The sun played at the edge of the western ridge.

She had almost made the garage when the blonde coerced lover, still carrying the bread knife, headed out to the car. Diving down behind the trunk of a tree, she watched the woman. The house looked quiet. The bedroom where she'd found the flip flops and snuck inside appeared empty. The other windows had no movement. Lady Erica likely stayed hidden, leaving any risk to her coerced.

The blonde woman opened the driver's door and got in. The wind picked up, sweeping leaves in its wake. It was an ominous sound in the silence.

Haddie's heart raced. She could stop the woman or make the entire car disappear. She couldn't let Lady Erica leave with Dad. As rough as the last use of her power had been, using it again might just kill her. *I'm not losing him.* It wouldn't be hard to roll out of sight and get into the back of the garage, but a hammer wouldn't stop the SUV from driving away.

The woman seemed to be searching for something. The engine didn't start. Keys? Those probably vanished with the guards ages ago. An hour ago?

Haddie waited a minute, then cringed when she tried to move and the leaves rustled under her. The wind still rattled trees in the woods. Moving in increments, she drew herself out of sight.

The back window was still open, and she climbed in and snuck back into the garage. The warmth and dull scent of oil reminded her of Dad's shop. Even Biff would be a welcome ally at this point. She ran to the window and watched the coerced woman digging through the glovebox. *Definitely keys.* Lady Erica and Dad were trapped here, unless Dad told them about Kiana and the RAV4. However, he didn't seem fully coerced yet. Perhaps his powers enabled him to resist. Either way, Lady Erica would either die or fix him.

When the lover finally gave up and got out of the Expedition, Haddie walked over to the bench and grabbed the hammer.

CHAPTER 43

Quietly, Aaron breathed in and out at the back of the garage. The sun hung on the edge of the ridge to his right. From the footsteps inside, he had to guess the blonde woman had gone into the garage after searching the vehicle. *What is she looking for? Weapons?*

He had hoped to find the keys himself, and barely escaped without her finding him digging through the SUV. He had waited for her to shut the car door, but she hadn't. Then he had heard the footsteps entering the other end of the empty garage. Earlier, he had climbed through a broken back window to get in. *There is nothing in there.* She searched for something though.

He faced the southern sky with the wall at his back. The wind blew in, bringing the storm and all its scents. Wide sprawling trees covered the ridge behind the house and garage. If he had a rifle, as Kiana had with Barbara Stevens, he would consider taking a shot.

What is my next move?

He had pondered shooting through a window and killing Lady Erica. He had found no sign of anyone in the house until the coerced woman had come out. *I procrastinated, searching the car.* It would have been useful had he found a key. A way to escape. The plan had been that the coerced would revert after he shot Lady Erica, but he had no guarantee.

Perhaps I am waiting for Haddie. Which one? He could sort out the issue of the two Haddies later. Why had neither one focused on the house? Did they have a plan? Certainly with as much song as he had heard today, a battle of power raged. Together, they might have overwhelmed Lady Erica and her coerced. *A phenomenal ability.* Why had she not gone back to the point before Thomas had been coerced?

The footsteps on the sidewalk startled him. They led away, back toward the house. He chanced a view around the edge of the building. The young woman returned toward the open door in the back, where she had come out. Her glow faded as she stepped inside and disappeared down a hall. If Lady Erica hid near the center of the house, he would have no idea how many protected her in there. *Including Thomas. It would be suicide to go inside.*

Leaning back against the garage wall, he took a deep breath. *I will have to sneak up to the porch and hope for a better vantage.* It would have to be one shot. He could hope that her coerced would become docile at that point. If not, he had the gun.

He stared at the leaves swaying in the new breeze. A moment to calm his nerves. For Haddie and her father, bravery seemed to come easily. Aaron drew in a deep breath. *I have to do this.*

CHAPTER 44

Thomas felt the weight of his skin. The Lady's scent hung fragrant in the air. Her beautiful face creased in a frown, and his heart tore, knowing that something frustrated her. He wanted to move, to speak, and let her know that he would take all her problems away. His body failed him. A tongue thick and rebellious barely shifted inside his mouth. *I love you, Lady.* The screaming part of his mind staggered him. He swayed, shifting a step.

The woman who had cut him came back inside. Her words were distorted in his ears and echoed long after her lips moved. She didn't matter.

The Lady, shining and bright, said something, but again the words were lost on him. She spoke to the shorter man. Together they looked at the tablet. What interested her?

I have to protect her. Again, his body swayed. Some traitorous part inside failed him and fought against his heart's desire. A knee folded and he caught himself from falling completely. Her look spurned him, chastising his weakness. She was disappointed with him. The pain of failure sucked his breath away.

I will do better.

PART 6

With our immortality and skills, we can initiate the justice they have prayed for and deserve.

CHAPTER 45

HADDIE STRODE across the backyard and stepped onto the grass beside the walk. The wind blustered, threatening the coming storm and rattling the trees at the ridge. Leaves loosened from the tree at the back of the house and danced in the air.

Through the kitchen window, Haddie couldn't see anyone moving inside. If Lady Erica and Dad stood close to where they'd been when she pushed herself back through time, she might see them when she got to the open door.

She held the hammer to her right side, the back of her thumb brushing across her exposed thigh. She ignored the tattered dress that flapped open ingloriously along her left side. Her bare foot made no sound in the grass, but the flip flop on the other made a slight squelch. *If I can surprise them, I might survive.* She kicked it off. Fingers clenching the wooden handle, she took a deep breath.

Lady Erica's voice sounded angry and scornful from inside. Slowing, Haddie stepped onto the porch. The hall was empty, and the only visible person lay at the front of the house under the dining table, close to where Haddie had been sitting initially. The woman curled away, toward the fireplace, but looked familiar. The yellow haze of coerced people filled the house. Most didn't move or shift.

Haddie's eyes adjusted to the dim light in the room. She could make out the foul scent from earlier, stronger now.

Dad's hand leaned forward and pressed against the floor. Haddie didn't hesitate. His cut cheek still looked wet. His eyes focused on the tile as he struggled to stand.

At the end of the hall, just to the left, the blonde lover who had cut him had her back to Haddie. She continued speaking, oblivious to any danger, ". . . inside the glovebox, or under the seats."

Lady Erica leaned forward and widened her eyes upon spotting Haddie.

Without any thought, Haddie brought the hammer up in a swing, catching the back of the blonde woman's skull.

Lady Erica stumbled back and began to sing.

Haddie rocked, hummed, and faltered a step. Her protection held. Humming hung in the air around her. The young lover crumpled to the tile. *She might die. What choice do I have?*

Gripping the hammer tightly, Haddie took the final step to the corner. Only one other coerced in the room shifted, a woman who leaned against the wall by the front double doors. She pawed the air with a limp hand. Dad hadn't gotten up yet. To Haddie's left, another coerced hung deeper in the corner where she had sent the blonde woman.

Startled, the short man juggled the tablet and gun. He stepped back, pressing against the two large wooden doors. His expression remained calm. He fumbled to switch the gun to his right hand while protecting the tablet at the same time. A poor choice.

With her weapon ready in the air after hitting the

blonde woman, Haddie swung. The impact hit his jaw, spraying blood from his mouth as he was flung back, against the doors. The gun and tablet dropped from his hands and clattered on the tile.

"Protect me." Lady Erica moved deeper into the dining room, but didn't stop pounding Haddie with her song.

A sunny sitting room with an outside door lay behind the woman. *I can't let her get in there.* The gun had landed closer to Lady Erica than Haddie.

Dad shifted to an awkward stance between them. Haddie's heart dropped at the sight of his eyes covered in the buzzing yellow haze.

A chair scraped at the table, and silverware tinkled to the floor. Far behind in the kitchen, someone, possibly the cook, dropped a metal pot or pan.

She remained focused on Dad and Lady Erica. Her only hope rested in his resistance to Lady Erica's power. She circled in a wide arc around Dad, holding the hammer at her right hip.

Lady Erica's lips pursed before she shouted, "Protect me!"

Dad lurched physically as if his legs intended to go in two different directions. The glow around his eyes buzzed angrily.

Fight it, Dad. The woman's song beat on Haddie, threatening to worm past her defenses. Others shifted in the room. They were far enough away that Haddie didn't need to turn, but she had little time left. Lady Erica's heel stepped on the threshold of the sunroom.

"Free him and I'll let you live." Haddie stepped forward, beside Dad.

The woman smiled and said, "Protect me."

Dad turned sharply toward Haddie and snarled. His tone filled the air.

Her protection barely held. The impact knocked her into the dining table behind her. Dishes smashed on tile. Silverware scattered. Lady Erica's song clashed with Dad's, an unbearable cacophony. The light appeared to dim. *He's turned against me.* Love had been unable to withstand Lady Erica's power.

The gun waited two yards away. *An impossible distance.* Dad's song clashed with Lady Erica's and pounded against Haddie. *I can't keep fighting this.* The hammer dropped from her hand. *Not that I could use it on Dad.* The thud of heavy metal and wood against tile echoed in her ears.

Her defenses wavered. Each of their songs nibbled away at it, drawing closer. *I'm going to lose.* Dad will kill me. Would he ever know? Feel guilt or remorse? *It's not his fault.* She would rather die than be coerced. In the end, she might have the better fate. Her hand pressed against the tile as her body dropped to the floor.

Dad's song stopped. Had he fought it? Her heart skipped, wanting to believe he loved her that much.

Trembling, Haddie raised her head. Weak, and needing protection, she wanted to believe his love was stronger than Lady Erica's power.

Facing away from her, Dad's song started to ring in the air. The glow still hung on his face. He faced a shape of someone standing in the hall.

"Stop it!" Aaron's voice shattered the discordance. His tone rang in the air with a tone reminiscent of Lady Erica's.

He stood, gun in hand, at the doorway. The light framed him in a dark silhouette. *Aaron, don't shoot Dad.*

"Shoot her," Haddie said, her voice a mere gasp. The muzzle of his weapon pointed at Dad dropped slowly.

Dad staggered. He stood between Lady Erica and Aaron. Dad's song had stopped. Aaron had freed him. The yellow haze was gone. *Thank you, Aaron.* Her heart jolted with hope, and she swallowed. She had her dad back. Safe. Wanting to hold him, she pushed up on her elbow. She hadn't wanted to give up on Dad, yet nothing she'd done had stopped the woman.

Could Lady Erica turn him back? Even now, the woman's song battered at Haddie. If she turned the focus back on Dad, what would it do?

Shoot her, Aaron, thought Haddie. Her fingers searched for the hammer.

Lady Erica had stopped her retreat when Dad joined her in attacking Haddie. Now, she took another step back into the sunroom. Sun shone glossy on the floor. The dark tile reflected it too brightly.

The gun that had shot Dad earlier in the day waited only a couple yards away. *I might be able to get it.* Dad straightened, his eyes clear. The yellow haze was gone, but he blinked, fighting some emotion.

Aaron did it. He could save Josh as well. They just had to stop Lady Erica. *Here and now.*

Dad spun, growling, and his song rang in the air. He focused not on Haddie, but on Lady Erica.

She shuddered under the attack, but managed to protect herself. Slightly different, but together, she sang both tones. Her protection and coercion hung in the air. It did not affect Dad; he did not become coerced again.

Aaron had crumpled to the floor and seemed to be sobbing.

Her fingers finding the handle of the hammer, Haddie

drew it into her palm. *You hold her, Dad.* Haddie had already killed innocents today. Lady Erica was hardly innocent. Crawling up to her knees, she felt a stabbing pain in her right calf.

She raised her eyebrows as she turned to find a fork stuck in her leg. Fingers of one of the coerced women who had managed to crawl across the floor lingered around it. Haddie slapped the woman's head with a glancing blow from the hammer. The pain spiked momentarily with the tug of the tines at her muscles when the woman's hand jerked away. The pain and the sensation made Haddie nauseous. Blood trickled dark red. It seemed surreal. *Pull it out.* Haddie put the hammer down and raised her hand tentatively.

Aaron screamed from the other side of the room. His gun fired, echoing in the confined space. Haddie's ears rung as she spun.

The cook staggered back, a large kitchen knife clattering almost silently to the tile. He hit the floor with a dull vibration through the floor. He twitched. Blood poured from his chest.

Lying on top of the lover, Aaron grabbed at the blood pouring out of his side. The coerced cook had managed to stab him. Likely Aaron had been stunned from the visions. He'd saved Dad. *And me.*

He had to survive.

First, they needed to stop Lady Erica.

Haddie's ears rang from the gunshot, dampening the two songs. She reached down and yanked the fork from her calf. It made no noise as it skidded across the tile.

In the back of the room, a shape crawled across the floor. Lady Erica's coerced were starting to come awake.

I can do this. The wound bled profusely, and her battles

had worn Haddie ragged, but she'd get the gun and finish the woman. Gritting her teeth, she looked up at Lady Erica, who had backed deeper into the sunroom.

Through the windows, the bright green grass stretched out under a sunny day. A misty light shone there. Rolling and folding in on itself it hung, as if watching. Haddie stared, transfixed. It was too intricate to be natural or even invite understanding. The ribbons of intertwining light seemed to reflect rather than illuminate. As soon as Haddie imagined form, it deepened and had underlying complexity.

Angels. Meg had called the lights "angels."

Haddie frowned and looked from Dad to Lady Erica. If it failed, she'd end up coerced. *I've got to take the chance.* Focusing on Lady Erica, she took a deep breath. Switching her tone, she released her protection, and sang in harmony with Dad's song.

The two notes knelled together like bells. The room seemed to waver and become insubstantial. Air seemed to warp shapes like heat off asphalt. She lost her distinct song in what they created.

Building into a crescendo, she felt the power pop. A physical force, but not air in the form of a shock wave. The world, perhaps gravity, seemed to shift suddenly. Haddie felt herself pushed back and falling away from Lady Erica. Lady Erica's shriek cut the air, then snipped short. Her body faded to a red mist that hung in the sunroom like a faint cloud. They had broken through Lady Erica's defenses and silenced her songs.

The world blurred. The ground reasserted itself. The sunlight seemed clear. The angel outside had disappeared as if it never existed. As her body convulsed in pain, Haddie couldn't stop herself from falling toward the brown tile.

CHAPTER 46

Haddie opened her eyes. The room had the stench of death. A round anchovy appetizer lay a few inches from her nose, settled in the grout between tiles. Someone sobbed.

Shivering, she remembered the war visions. They seemed like nightmares, the vivid ones that would keep her awake at night.

Aaron. She lifted her head, then opened her mouth in silent pain. Her skin and joints burned. Movement caused awareness of everywhere she touched the tile or clothes touched her.

The sunroom seemed bright. The dark shadowed area between the back hall and the bright sitting room appeared to move. Dad's back. He hunched over Aaron. Kneeling, he spoke quietly.

The sobbing came from behind Haddie, around the dining tables. More than one of the coerced cried or stirred, but they didn't seem to threaten.

"Dad?" Haddie's voice croaked in a bare whisper. How bad had Aaron been hurt?

Dad didn't respond, except to make a gesture for her to

come to him.

Aaron's dying. Sucking in a breath, she leveraged herself onto her elbow. Her right knee, pressing against the tile, resisted holding her weight. Haddie set her eyes on Aaron's extended legs. He wore his usual jeans. Not stonewashed or bleached, but the dark blue, new kind.

He had risked himself, despite everything he'd ever said, and saved Dad. *Saved me.* She had treated him horribly over the past few days. *Ever since Josh.* Why had he chosen to help now? He'd come when he planned on leaving. Then he'd fixed Dad, when he'd refused to try on Josh. She flushed, embarrassed, and crawled toward Dad.

Aaron lay against the wall and the legs of the blonde woman. Her face still glowed, so she was alive and coerced. Dad had found a towel and wadded it against Aaron's side. Little of it was white anymore, and blood had soaked into the waist of his jeans. *He's lost too much blood.* His eyes blinked constantly. His skin looked pale, and he took rapid, shallow breaths. "How?" he asked.

"Does she survive the visions?" Dad's quiet voice sounded calm. She recognized the tone from when she'd been hurt after the raves. They must have been having a conversation.

Aaron nodded, then grimaced as if he might cry.

Haddie felt tears well up. "I don't, not completely. They haunt me." She spoke knowing he was dying in front of her. If Dad thought he could save him, he would be trying. It reminded her of when Mula died. "There's so many now." Her voice broke with a sob. Aaron needed her to be calm. "I can't think about it when I use my power."

There had to be something they could do. How could they just sit there and wait for him to die? She sucked in a sob. Lifting one hand off the floor, she wiped her eyes.

Dad looked at her. "Do you think you can get him some water?" When Mula had died, they could only make her dog more comfortable. *That's what Dad's doing now.*

Tears blurring her vision, she nodded, though she questioned her ability to get on her feet.

"Wait," Aaron forced the word.

Her chest ached, but she sniffled and said, "Yes?"

"Thank you for . . ." He winced and huffed in a breath. "I was alone." The last word seemed to take all his breath.

Haddie dropped her head and let her tears fall. Was he thanking her for friendship? *I've been a horrible friend.* She'd called him terrible names, and still he saved her dad.

She had to say something. Wiping her face, she sucked in a deep breath. "Thank you for saving Dad. I don't know what I would have done."

"Haddie." Dad's voice told her there was no need to continue.

She sobbed and looked up. Aaron stared at her, lifelessly. Sagging to the ground, she let herself cry. Regret and guilt wracked her. Dad put his hand on her back, and she leaned toward him. This had been her fault, all along. Focused only on Josh, she'd been willing to drag them all into this mess. *Selfish.* Kiana had a broken leg and Dad had been shot. She could have lost all of them.

"Kiana," Haddie said. She choked trying to say more.

Dad turned toward her, his eyebrows drawing close. "Where is she?"

"She broke her leg. She's down at the road." Haddie sniffled, rubbing her eyes.

Dad's expression grew dark, then distant. For a moment, he glanced away. He shook his head. "How long ago?"

"An hour?" Haddie shrugged.

"We need to get to her." He winced and stood. "I promised Aaron I wouldn't leave him here. Can you help?"

Dad kept his left arm still, by his side. From the placement of the bandage, the bullet had gone through his upper arm. It would be a while before he'd be carrying anything with it. She doubted she had the strength to carry Aaron down the hill to the RAV4. Walking seemed a challenge.

"Don't suppose you have Biff on the way?"

Dad shook his head. "We can go down and get her and drive back up."

She followed his glance across the room. One of the coerced women attempted to stand.

Haddie smiled. "Unless you want to hotwire the Expedition out back."

He nodded. "I forgot about that. My memory is a bit foggy." Dad offered a hand to pull her up. "Best we stick together."

Grimacing, Haddie stood with his help. He leaned down and took the gun from Aaron's hand, checked it, and stuck it in his suit pocket. His bandage needed to be tied properly.

"Do you have one of your medical friends near here?" Haddie reached down and grabbed the tablet. It had a slight crack at one corner. She'd killed the man who had carried it. His glow had faded, and he lay motionless in the corner.

The blonde woman lay on the dead man's legs; she might make it. Haddie had killed people today. Again. The initial horror she'd felt over it wasn't there. It disgusted her, and she hoped the blonde lover survived, but they had threatened her family and friends. She began to understand her dad's callous reaction to it. *I don't want to be like this.*

Wincing, she made it to the gun that had been used to shoot Dad. She could smell the death coming from the sunroom. The remains of Lady Erica spread across the floor. How long had the woman's residue been rotting there? *No wonder the place stunk.*

The fork wound hurt more than she'd expected. She hobbled after Dad to hotwire the SUV and left the gun and tablet on the front passenger seat. *Terry will have a blast with the device.*

The few coerced who had awakened numbly watched as she and Dad returned for Aaron. The cook's blood had created a wide slick that they had to maneuver over carefully. None of the women made any attempt to stop them. *What will happen to them now that Lady Erica is gone? What is happening to Josh?*

They managed to get Aaron's body into the back of the Expedition. A rental. Dad insisted they go back into the house and retrieve anything they'd handled, including the hammer and phone. Unable to determine which she had touched from the scattered silverware on the floor, Haddie ended up with a handful in a garbage bag. The coerced didn't stop her. They barely seemed aware of her.

The storm to the north had moved closer, roiling over the hills. It would be raining within the hour. Cold wind blustered to the top parking lot. She drove them down the hill, stopping midway. A blue Honda Accord was parked where the bus had been.

"Keep driving. They won't know to stop us."

Haddie nodded and continued slowly. A coerced woman sat in the driver's seat. She didn't even look at them as they drove by. Absently, her hands held the steering wheel as the engine idled. *Is this how Josh was right now?* Haddie let out a breath. They needed to get Kiana and Dad looked at, stitched up and splinted, or whatever was necessary.

CHAPTER 47

Haddie stopped the Expedition in the road where she'd left Kiana. The woman hid easily among the trees in the growing shade of the ridge. The RAV4 sat down the road, partially obscured by the brush.

Dad jumped out before Haddie shifted the car into park.

The air smelled of rain. The wind tugged at the uppermost trees, spraying leaves down into the woods around Kiana. She tugged on her ear, searching Haddie's face. *What is she worried about?* Dad knelt beside her. Haddie hobbled toward them favoring her calf.

"Where is it broken?" he asked.

Kiana's lips pressed together in a light grimace. She seemed about to speak, then her face tightened again. Her eyes flicked across Dad's face, searching.

"It's okay, Kiana." Haddie smiled. "Aaron fixed Dad. Lady Erica's gone." Her throat thickened and she swallowed. "Aaron didn't make it. One of the coerced stabbed him." She reached back to her neck, her hair wadded in a tangle.

Dad put his hand on Kiana's shoulder. She flinched, then searched Haddie's face. "Why didn't you know that Aaron was here?"

She snorted. "Yeah, I must have sounded crazy. I came down right after Dad had been coerced, then I pushed myself back in time and called you, then came down when the demon broke your leg."

Kiana seemed to work through the comments, nodding slowly. "Where's Aaron? He wouldn't want to be left here."

Dad gestured toward the SUV. He studied her outstretched right leg and the jeans. "Where's the break? How bad?"

"Tibia, maybe fibula."

"Clean break?"

Kiana tilted her head. "Don't know. Not poking through the skin."

"That's always good. We still need to get it checked right away." He looked up at Haddie. "Can you bring the RAV4 up here? I'll drive Aaron, and you take Kiana. I'll get Crow to meet us and help with Aaron's body."

Kiana grimaced as she reached into the jean pockets. "The big guy? From Boise?"

Dad nodded, holding out his right hand. "He should be in the city by now."

Throwing the keys directly to Haddie, Kiana nodded toward Dad's left arm. "What happened?"

"Through and through. Muscle. I'll be fine."

"Maybe you'll have a real scar."

Haddie walked downhill with the keys. Her scars healed too well, so Dad's likely did. Kiana probably thought he had none. *She doesn't know.* Obviously, he wouldn't want to tell her. *Would David notice my lack of scars?* He'd known she'd been hurt before, stitches even. She looked down at her hands where Harold Holmes had burned her less than a year ago. *Almost gone.*

The first drops of rain sprinkled the windshield as they loaded Kiana into the back seat of the RAV4. Dad was soaked by the time he had her settled, called Crow with Kiana's cell, and climbed into the stolen Expedition. Haddie followed him down the road, dying for something to drink. Her water bottle sat in her hotel room. Would they even be heading back? *Probably not. I need something to wear.* The ruined dress left her hip and side exposed.

Dad led with the RAV4, and they'd only driven down to the first set of buildings when he pulled off to the side.

"What's wrong?" Kiana asked.

Haddie leaned up to the windshield, peering through the heavy downpour. The bus had been abandoned on a side road. A Ford F250 parked beside it, and the door to the bus hung open. A young man with a red cap jumped out with bottles in both hands. They were looting the bus. *Where is the driver?* He'd likely gone for help.

Dad pulled back out into the road and waited.

They could get their burners back. She sighed. Some local law enforcement would eventually be here. *I don't want to have to explain.* She pulled in behind Dad and they continued along the road.

Kiana spoke loudly over the thumping wipers and the heavy rain on the roof. "We need to call Terry. I got worried after the last time you talked to me. I thought they'd coerced you as well."

They'd have to tell him about Aaron. Haddie swallowed. "Okay."

Dad led them, driving at a reasonable speed. The turns had slowed him down, but now they were on a fairly straight downhill grade. Houses filled in flatter areas with trucks and cars parked around them or on the side of the road. A Chevy Blazer with a police or sheriff insignia passed. *Heading for the bus?*

Rain pounded against the roof, filling the silence before Kiana spoke. "Terry. We're out."

Haddie waited, unable to hear even a murmur of Terry's voice over the storm.

"She's fine. Aaron was able to clear Thomas. He's fine."

Ahead, Dad indicated right as the road ended at a stop sign. He waited to turn until they pulled up behind. The RAV4's headlights lit the sheets of rain and the edge of the fields. A car ahead of them had their flashers on.

"Patch it through to the car." Kiana sounded frustrated.

Haddie connected the phone to the RAV4. "Hey, Terry." The surrounding neighborhood turned abruptly into suburbia. Houses and side streets took the place of rural fields.

"How do I know it's you? Or you, but not coerced?"

"I'm looking in the mirror now, and I don't have a yellow haze."

Kiana chuckled in the back.

"You could be lying."

"I could, but take my word for it. From what I saw, few people are able to even sit or talk after she got done with them. Dad was no exception." Haddie swallowed. "I do have something to tell you." A stream of headlights burned through the rain, heading toward her.

"What?" Terry asked.

A caravan of black SUVs, mostly Fords, passed. Haddie almost touched the brakes as she recognized passing glimpses of yellow haze and orange eyes. They were on their way to Lady Erica's getaway. They didn't slow or seem to recognize the rented Expedition that Dad drove.

"Uhm, yeah." There was no good way to say it. "Aaron saved Dad, pushed the coercion right out of him, but Lady Erica had coerced everyone else there. One of them killed Aaron." Haddie watched her rearview mirror, but the cavalcade made no hint of stopping or following them. They couldn't know whether she or Dad had come off the mountain road.

"That doesn't make me trust you more."

It would be worse if he knew Aaron could see the haze; it would sound suspicious that he didn't survive. "Well, be cautious with me. I'll understand. I do have something that I need you to look at."

Terry took a moment to respond. "What's that?"

"I have the tablet that Lady Erica's attendant kept with him. He was very protective over it. I think it's important." She glanced back at the mirrors. There were no lights behind her. "Lady Erica is gone. We'll have to see if it helps Josh."

"Very cool. When will you be back?" His suspicious tone disappeared.

"We need to make some stops. We have Aaron's body. Kiana has a broken leg, and Dad's been shot."

"Jeez, Haddie. What can I do?" He grunted. "Nothing. Obviously. I'm sure the FBI are watching. How about you? Are you okay?"

Dad put on a blinker and Haddie slowed. "Ruined my dress. Some lady put a fork in me."

"So, you're done?"

Haddie raised her eyebrows. "I've got to go. We're stopping."

"Take care, Buckaroo. Call me later."

Haddie hung up. She'd call Liz on her regular cell, once she found out why Dad stopped.

They pulled into a gas station, and Dad waved them to the pumps while he parked on the outer edge of the lot. Jogging through the rain, he came up to her driver's door. "Phone?" He put out his palm. "Turn your engine off. We'll gas up here." He looked at her dress. "Stay in the car. I'll pay and pump." He had dress pants and shoes on, though shirtless with a bloody bandage wrapped around his arm.

"Are you sure, Dad?" *I'd be no less obvious with my ass hanging out.*

He snorted and walked away. Dialing the phone, he headed for the store. She hadn't thought to ask for something to drink. Despite the rain, she could see him make a quick sweep through the store. He put on a T-shirt and threw an extra one over his shoulder. In on hand, he grabbed two gallon jugs. Carrying everything else he bought in one bag, he walked out wearing a black T-shirt that read, "Mt. Diablo Accomplished." The cut on his cheek appeared little more than an angry pink line with a red center.

He dropped the pile outside her passenger side and opened her car with his good arm. Dad tossed her a matching T-shirt. "It's going to get chilly." She eyed the water he placed on her passenger seat as she slid the shirt over her torn dress. "What are we —"

"Crow's meeting us here. There's a grocery store behind us with a big parking lot. He's going to take care of Aaron's body and the SUV." He glanced back at Kiana. "How are you doing? Feeling okay?" He tossed a small bottle to her that rattled of pills.

"As good as can be expected."

"I'll get us to a friend of mine in about an hour. He's got a portable x-ray that he uses for his animals. We'll get you in better shape."

"And you," Kiana teased.

Dad nodded. "And me."

Another vet. Dad collected medical connections like he did identities and properties. He used caution in every aspect of his life, but this time he'd even urged Haddie into the situation. Haddie had been happy to go along with it. Aaron had died. She'd nearly lost Dad. However, they had stopped the coercion. *Possibly freed Josh.*

Dad nodded at her dash. "Open the gas tank."

She leaned down and pressed the button. "Aaron's phone," Haddie offered.

He nodded. "I'll go through his clothes."

Haddie teared as he walked around the car to the pump. Aaron had sacrificed himself for Dad. She looked forward to getting back to Eugene, but it felt wrong to leave him to Crow. *What choice do I have?*

She needed more information before she accepted Crow handling Aaron. *I'm not letting them dump his body.*

CHAPTER 48

THOMAS REACHED into the middle console for his water and checked on Kiana sleeping behind the driver's seat. He sat across from her, trying to sleep as well. Her color looked good. The Rolls Ghost had been a smooth ride. Crow had been lucky to rent one. The interior smelled like antiseptic and fried take out. Kiana's leg had swelled in the bindings of the splint; she'd get a cast on it once the swelling went down. *If I can keep her off of it.*

Crow laughed from the driver's seat. "We're at Crow Road." The car slowed to the intersection. Fields spread in every direction, backed by pines and oaks bright green in the midday sun.

Haddie looked at the street sign and chuckled, which only encouraged Crow to laugh and thump on the steering wheel.

Kiana blinked and straightened her head. She smiled when she saw Thomas watching her. Despite everything they'd gone through, she kept her heart open. "Where are we?"

"West side of Eugene." He leaned toward her. Reaching

across, he laid his hand on top of hers. Slowly, she grasped the tips of his fingers

She nodded. "I'd still rather go with you. Might make Terry more comfortable."

Thomas shrugged. *My least concern is Terry's sensibilities.* Haddie had been unrelenting about a burial for Aaron. The man deserved a sendoff, but there were unacceptable risks. Like any good compromise, no one was happy.

He checked the time on the burner Crow had bought him. *Just after noon.* Crow's people would likely bury the body in the next hour if they kept to schedule. He had another contact monitoring the traffic into the rural area who wouldn't see what Crow's people were doing, but they would identify any additional people who might follow. *Too many risks.*

The letter had put him in an aggressive mood. He'd acted rashly, endangering Haddie and leaving Aaron dead and Kiana injured. His emotions had gotten him into trouble over the centuries. *I should have learned by now.* There were too many loose ends. He and Haddie had been seen by the models and the coerced applicants. Their burners were in the bus, with fingerprints. He couldn't be sure they'd gotten all their fingerprints from the house. And, he had a body to dispose of, which meant involving too many people and risking information leaking out.

I can't fight these people like this. Whatever new information he learned, he'd have to keep from Haddie. He wouldn't involve her again. She could still be at risk if one clue led them back to her identity. Extra people had already been assigned to stake out her workplace. *I reacted to that damnable letter.*

"What are you frowning about?" Kiana asked.

Haddie looked back from the passenger seat.

Thomas shook his head. "We're not hobbling you up to my van. Neither of us are in any shape for that." He gestured toward Haddie. "We keep to the plan. I pick up the van and meet up with Terry. That will be risky enough. You two will stay with Crow, and we'll meet at the grave."

Kiana shrugged and squeezed his fingers.

One benefit of the funeral, it kept Haddie from heading home immediately. Any activity at her apartment would flag his people.

Crow turned the corner onto Oak Hill Drive.

Thomas grabbed his bottle of water. "Haddie, move to the back when I get out."

"Planning on it."

She probably wants to chat with Kiana. The little time they'd had at the vet's was spent sleeping, and they'd slept during most of the ride up I-5. Haddie's experience still concerned him. It had been uncomfortable enough to learn of Kiana's months pushed backward in time. How had Haddie decided to risk that? *I might have, in her place.*

He took a tight breath when he considered how close he'd come to killing her. *I'm not going to think about it.* Losing himself to Lady Erica had been the singularly most terrifying moment of his life. Shoving the memory away, he focused on the risks ahead of them.

Crow brought the Rolls to a stop where the road curved and two others intersected it. Kiana motioned Thomas to her for a kiss before she would let him get out.

Thomas grimaced as he climbed out. The stitches felt tight. "Be careful." The hot air hung heavy on the street, smelling of pine and manure.

Haddie hobbled out wearing sweatpants that covered most of her scrapes and cuts. Her arms and face were nearly black with purpura; she'd pushed herself too far using her powers. The vet couldn't do much, but suggested she keep the calf clean and change the bandages at night and again in the morning. At least her wounds weren't too bad. *I feel responsible enough for Kiana's leg.*

Sweating immediately as he began walking, Thomas trekked up the road toward Darren Robertson's house. *I'll miss this house.* The hillside property would be going on the market in the next day or two. No point in keeping it, not with Kiana moving in with Meg and Sam. One of his people had already cleared out the house, and plastic bags would be inside the Ford Transit.

He had to roll down the windows of the van despite the shade of the oak. It smelled like chemicals with the plastic bags baking inside. No one moved on Darren's property as Thomas drove out and headed into Eugene. Stopping at an intersection, he texted an exclamation point to Terry. His next text went to his contact.

Once he received an all clear, he headed for 11th Avenue and the carwash.

Terry waited where he'd been told under the broad tree. As Thomas pulled up beside the vacuum, Terry opened the side door and climbed in, sitting on the floor by the plastic bags. "Hey, T. This is fun."

"You parked at the auto body shop?" Thomas began backing out.

"Yep, and walked through the dollar store. Didn't come out 'til I got your text. We're good." The man grinned foolishly, making him look more like a kid than a college student.

"Then we're on our way. Keep down until we get out of Eugene."

Terry stretched out, ankles crossed, and put his arms behind his head. "You got it, Captain."

The man acted the fool, but Thomas knew he was bright. What he'd managed to dig up overnight, some of the best people Thomas could hire would take a week, if they found it at all. That had also led to his trouble with the FBI. Perhaps he'd become more careful. Haddie needed good people. The way she treated others — the way she cared for them, usually led to loyal friends. Now, if he could just keep them, and himself, from running headlong into disaster, he might figure out who was behind the letter. That tablet would be key, and Terry would be the man for that.

CHAPTER 49

Haddie enjoyed the ride in the Rolls-Royce, but hadn't liked the idea of strangers driving the RAV4 from the vet's. Kiana looked much more comfortable in the larger vehicle, stretched out in a luxurious back seat that accommodated her leg and brace. The seat smelled like Dad's antiseptic from his bandage, and the heat from opening the doors forced the air conditioner's fan to kick too high.

"Can I borrow your phone?" Haddie asked. She couldn't bring herself to use Aaron's.

Kiana nodded and pointed to it in the console between the seats. "Terry?"

Haddie shook her head and unplugged the burner from the charger. "Liz." They'd be driving through Eugene for a bit, so cell service would be strong. There was a lot to explain to Liz. She peered through tinted windows as they drove down 11th.

She texted Liz with her regular cell, "Quiz me."

They'd worked up the code after her last change in burners. *Who would think I'd be doing this?*

Liz texted back, "Lead acetate, lactic acid, potassium dichromate, and sodium citrate."

Looking up the formulas on the web, Haddie altered the numbers Ozones counted as a zeros, and any extra numbers were used up as elevens in the beginning and repeats of the tenth number at the end. Liz, of course, had come up with it. "Wrong," she texted Liz's new number.

Kiana's burner rang immediately. "Hey," Haddie answered.

"I expected your call last night. What happened to your other burner? Are you okay?" Liz's concerned tone matched her rapid questions.

"It didn't go well. Aaron's dead."

"Shit, Haddie. How?"

Because we jumped in without thinking it through. "Lady Erica coerced Dad, and Aaron risked himself to fix him. Dad's okay, but one of Lady Erica's coerced stabbed Aaron. He bled out." A flush rose up to her ears. Each time Haddie thought it through, she thought about how badly she had treated him. *Like a coward. He wasn't a coward.*

"Damn."

The worst part over, Haddie moved into the topic she wanted to discuss with Liz. "I pushed myself back in time."

"Like you did with Kiana?"

"Yeah."

"What did it feel like?" Liz asked.

Painful. "Nothing. Just — blip — I was in the same place in a different time."

"Same as Kiana." Liz hummed on the other end of the phone. "Didn't get me any blood."

Haddie smiled. "I did." Dad and the vet had been rather puzzled, but had eventually agreed to pack and send a vial to Liz's address. "It should be there today. Some medical shipping or courier. I didn't pay attention."

"To my house? It's a hundred degrees out. Well, in the eighties, but still. I'm cutting out early. I feel this cold kicking back up suddenly." Liz coughed audibly and loud. "Any weird symptoms? Are you okay?"

"As good as can be expected." Haddie extended her purple dotted hand. "I'm going to be fine."

"Lady Erica?"

"Dead. Gone."

"Josh?" Liz asked.

"Don't know." Haddie sighed. *I failed.*

"Are you at work? No, you're driving back."

"Called in last night, left a message on Toby's answering machine."

"Damn, doesn't sound good. I'm sorry. Where are you? When will you see Josh?"

Haddie had used the rash as an excuse, so heading into work with heavy makeup wouldn't be a surprise. She imagined Lady Erica's white painted skin. "I might go in tomorrow. I'll let you know what I find out about Josh."

"I can check in on you tonight." Liz sounded hopeful. It had been a few days since they'd seen each other, before her cold had started.

"Maybe. We're doing a simple funeral for Aaron. I'm not sure what the plan is afterward."

"Call me?"

"If I get service out there." Haddie took a deep breath and hung up. Dad had valid concerns that she — they'd been identified. Fingerprints were on her cell phone, at the least. If they were lucky, the local kids stole them before the police arrived.

What had happened when the coerced and demons

arrived – would they have stopped at the bus, or headed straight up to Lady Erica's house? How much sway did this person who pulled the strings have? They had some control of the FBI. Terry and Aaron had always complained that the removal of the demon photos was a government conspiracy. How deep did their organization go?

Haddie jacked Kiana's burner into the charger.

Kiana looked less pale. "So, the first time I saw you was after you jumped back in time. How long had you been there?"

Haddie shook the images of demons attacking local sheriffs out of her head. "Over an hour. It took me a while to make it to the phone and call you. Then I snuck downhill to wait for you, but I picked a spot too far down. I didn't think you'd get that close. You'd left the RAV4 before I got up there. Then, well — the guards and the demons happened."

Kiana gestured, as if understanding something. "I couldn't figure out the phone call. It happened after Thomas had been coerced by Lady Erica - at least to you. Though in my time, and your first time, you and Thomas hadn't left the hotel yet. The two calls came so close together, I thought it had just happened." She leaned back and closed her eyes. "It's starting to come together now. Not all of it."

Haddie nodded and looked out the window at Eugene as they drove through it. She'd tried to explain, multiple times, but she had no clock or phone to know the exact timing. The men she'd killed, Sandy, and the little blonde lover stung at each retelling. She couldn't know if the two women had survived. *I don't want to hurt people.* Each time she came to the points when Dad had been coerced or had tried to kill her, it became difficult to focus on the timeline. She could blame Lady Erica, but they had chosen to infiltrate. That woman's death didn't bring the same remorse as the innocents she coerced. *She'd almost taken Dad.* What had happened to Josh, now that she was dead?

The buildings blurred by, and Haddie shut her eyes. She woke as the Rolls turned onto a dirt road. Gratefully she shook off the nightmare of Sandy cresting the top of a trench armed with a kitchen knife and wearing a dirty black uniform.

Kiana shifted up. "Are we here?"

Crow leaned back, but kept his eyes on the forest road. "Almost."

Tall brush crumpled under the Rolls-Royce Ghost and feathered across the bottom. The pines were widely spaced, giving ample view of the hills and slopes around them. The air in the car became spiced with the crushed plants. Haddie leaned forward. They weren't the first to come onto the path. Tires had pushed ruts into the fresh green grass and bushes.

Their trail ended at a slab of weather-stained cement in a small clearing. A midden of wood and debris rotted in the back, but vines and brush had taken over all but the concrete. On Kiana's side, pines dotted a slight incline where orange flowers clustered in the more open, sunlit areas. On Haddie's side, thick brush surrounded an indent that could have been a stream.

Crow shifted into park and left the engine running. "We'll wait for Tempest here."

Haddie lasted all of fifteen minutes. "I want to go see."

Crow shrugged and turned off the car.

The air smelled of baking sap and fresh pine. No breeze cut the heat. The sun made it through the needles of the canopy, filtered and speckling across the ground.

Haddie wore the padded slippers Crow had bought, but

she cringed as she stepped out. Her feet, bandaged and clean, still felt raw. It had been two hours since their last stop, right before dropping Dad off. The tinkling water made her regret sleeping the whole way and not getting Crow to stop. Mosquitoes immediately found her and buzzed in her ears.

Crow moved to the trunk of the luxury sedan and pulled out a wheelchair for Kiana. "We're just up that hill." He gestured to the slight incline with orange wildflowers.

Haddie paused to help with Kiana, but Crow waved her on. Crow was square bodied; where Dad had height, he had thick tattooed arms that easily navigated the wheels through the pine needles.

Aaron's grave was obvious and unpretentious. He would rest here unknown to all but them. *I'll come out.* A rectangle of dirt was cut from the top of a sparsely grown rise. She could see a mountaintop to the south. It looked so empty and plain. As Kiana was rolled to the top, Haddie headed back for wildflowers. When she had a solid handful of tiny orange and red flowers with almost orchid-like blossoms, some with roots, she returned to Aaron's grave and planted them in the center. She had no idea where his head or feet lay.

Twenty minutes they sat in the heat and insects, waiting for Dad and Terry. She had no reception, so she only knew they arrived when the white Ford van rolled through the brush below.

Terry ran up the hillside and nearly tackled Haddie with a hug. "I can't believe this." He grimaced at her face when he released. Kiana received a similar hug. When Terry looked at Crow, the large man raised an eyebrow. Terry returned to Haddie and tried to put his arm around her shoulder, but he was a couple inches too short.

Dad made it to the top, looked at the mountain in the distance, and nodded. "He's got a good view.' He gestured to the flowers. "Aquilegia." Kneeling beside Kiana, he held her hand.

He let a minute pass before he cleared his throat. "I guess we should all say something." A nearby bird replied with a sad call. "So, I'll start. Aaron, I underestimated you from the start. You had courage to spare. Thank you for saving our lives. You were a good man. You deserved better than this."

Terry let go of Haddie and rubbed his hands together. "Doc, you were amazing." He swallowed and shook his head. His tone changed to a lighter expression. "Doc A. Survived by his friend and mentor, Terry the Maestro of the Meta, his fearless leader, Buckaroo, and comrade in arms, Special K — Doc you will always be in our hearts and minds." Despite his light-hearted attempt, Terry's voice cracked at the end.

Kiana had tears in her eyes, and a lone streak down her cheek. "Rest in peace, Aaron."

His grave, brown dirt mixed with pine needles, cut a ragged rectangle in the forest. The flowers looked wilted, if bright. He had no family that would miss him. The only others who would know of his passing were the people on the internet who followed his anonymous posts. Terry would likely let them know.

Aaron would be alone. *Some random property. Likely Dad's.* Aaron was due better.

Haddie shook her head against the bugs, but refused to wipe away the tears. Aaron warranted them. "I'm going to try and quote from Kahlil Gibran's 'On Death' from one of Dad's books."

"*The Prophet,*" Dad added.

"I don't remember all of it, but there's a couple lines that might fit:

For life and death are one, even as the river and the sea are one.

In the depth of your hopes and desires lies your silent knowledge of the beyond;

And like seeds dreaming beneath the snow your heart dreams of spring.

Trust the dreams, for in them is hidden the gate to eternity."

A breeze gusted between them, scattering pine needles.

Dad cleared his throat. "It ends with:

Only when you drink from the river of silence shall you indeed sing.

And when you have reached the mountain top, then you shall begin to climb.

And when the earth shall claim your limbs, then shall you truly dance."

Haddie sucked in a sob. *You didn't die in vain.* He had saved Dad. Aaron had only wanted to understand the demons, perhaps stop them. That was what she would do for him.

HADDIE WOKE on the couch as Rock sniffed her face with wet whiskers. Dad's house smelled like eggs and pancakes with a hint of coffee. Louis clattered on tile in the kitchen. She opened an eye and scratched Rock's ear as he nuzzled. Dad hadn't bothered with much furniture in the living room. A couple soft chairs on each side of a table sat across the room. He hadn't put many books on the bookshelf that was built into the wall.

"Tea?" Sam asked.

Haddie groaned and tilted her head toward her friend. Sam smiled, leaning on the kitchen doorway. She wore her trans pin on a pale blue blouse. Dad and Kiana ate at the kitchen table, a heavy country piece that stretched down the long room.

"Sure, I'll be right there." Haddie winced, sitting up and rubbing at her eyes. "What time is it?"

"Eight. We just got back from checking on the kennel. The door closing probably woke you." Her ferret zipped under her legs to duck behind Haddie's couch.

Haddie stumbled toward the bathroom. She'd have to

get back to Eugene today. Dad had the RAV4 nearby, but he'd have to drop her off. Her face still looked horrifying. The purpura speckled so thickly that she looked mottled and old. *I need a break.* She wouldn't let Aaron down; Terry already had theories about where to look for the source of the demons. He hoped the tablet would yield some answers. They let him take it with him after he promised to be careful.

Sam sat at the kitchen table with Dad and Kiana, though she didn't eat. A plate of pancakes waited for Haddie along with hot tea melting in a glass of ice. Meg sat on the floor petting Rock while Louis jumped around them both. Dad hadn't put his arm in a sling, but he held it stiffly by his side.

"You slept well," Dad said.

Haddie sipped the fresh tea, her lips chilling on the ice over the warm liquid. "I crashed. What did I sleep, twelve hours?"

Dad nodded.

Haddie's pancakes were still warm, but the butter didn't really melt. The sweet syrup kept them moist. Suddenly famished, she began wolfing through the plate.

"When you get fed and dressed, we'll drive out to your car." Dad grabbed his and Kiana's plates and headed for the sink.

Kiana smiled, somewhat awkwardly, and grabbed the crutches that were leaning on the chair beside her. "You'll call, once you get settled back there?" She wanted to know about Josh.

Haddie nodded. "Of course. I'm going to miss you."

Her smile broadening, Kiana said, "I'm going to miss you too. We've come a long way together."

Dad had moved her in. It would be safer than the hillside house. Out here in the woods, they would be together. *I'm not jealous.* There were uncomfortable feelings, but she'd already gotten used to Dad being away. Haddie couldn't imagine being able to live with David. Her blotchy hands stabbed one of the last pieces from the stack of pancakes.

It hadn't always been like this with the coerced and demons. This past year had been unusual. She still had the demons to worry about, but maybe the coerced had been released. She'd find out when she got around Josh again.

Dad helped Kiana toward the back bedrooms, leaving Haddie at the table with Sam. Pulling up her regular cell, she checked for any messages from David. Detective Cooper had left two since Monday morning. At first, she'd worried they were about San Francisco, but they were the usual query about Dad's location. Haddie kept up the pretense that Dad still biked in the mountains. *Nothing new.*

"I miss you," Sam said.

"I miss you too." Haddie swallowed. Her emotions were still raw. Losing Aaron had hit her harder than she would have imagined.

"You're okay, after this trip?"

Haddie nodded. Sam never asked about the details, but she always cared about the aftermath. "I believe I did the right thing," Haddie said.

"That's what matters. You care, Haddie. That may get you in some tough spots, but I can't imagine you not trying, no matter the consequences."

Aaron. All those innocents who had been coerced. *Consequences.* "I still question the outcomes."

"That's good, isn't it? If you didn't care about the repercussions, what would that make you?"

A monster. She still felt like one sometimes, ever since the raves. *I do care.* "You're right. I just wish could avoid some of it and still do the right thing."

Sam got up and grabbed Haddie's plate and glass. "Another tea?"

"Yes." Even out in the woods at Dad's new farm, it felt like home when she hung out with Sam. There would be plenty of time to get back and check on Josh. *What will I find?*

Meg stood up and walked over to Haddie. "The angels were right."

Haddie felt a chill climb up her neck. She'd seen one. They weren't just Meg's imagination. "About what?"

"Harmony." Meg laughed. She seemed pleased with herself. "They're very interested in you."

The hairs on Haddie's neck prickled. "Why?"

Meg shrugged and tried to pet Louis as he raced past. "I don't know. They don't think about that."

"Where did you see them last?"

Sam brought back a fresh glass of tea, steam drifting off the top. "Yesterday, at the kennel. I can always tell when she sees them now. I told you that you were doing the right thing. Why would angels follow you otherwise?" She wore a wry smirk, as if humoring one or both of them.

Haddie drank her tea. Meg chased Louis. *I need to talk with Dad about Meg's angels.* Had he ever seen them? They had been the inspiration for her to sing in harmony with Dad. Without that, they might not have defeated Lady Erica.

Dad stepped back into the kitchen and raised an eyebrow. "We leaving?"

She groaned and finished her tea. "Let me get dressed."

An hour later, when Sam and Meg had left on their

four-wheeler for the kennel, Haddie broached the subject of angels with Dad. He couldn't remember seeing anything like what she described.

"I'm concerned we're imagining something based a construct Meg is using to cope." He rubbed his hair back and climbed up into the Ford Transit.

"I've seen something." The last image, out on the lawn, she could remember clearly. It defied explanation, but she'd seen something.

He nodded, starting up the van. "I'll be more open-minded to it. Maybe if I don't think of them as angels, it would be easier. The religious connotations make it difficult for me."

Rock stretched up to the console to watch the road as they drove through Dad's forest. Once they got to paved asphalt, they passed the kennel. Haddie couldn't be sure when she'd get to see Sam or Meg again. *Or Kiana*. She sighed, pushing the heavy weight from her chest. More and more of the people she cared about were moving out of Eugene. She still had Terry and Liz.

Her RAV4 waited just down the road, parked behind a deserted house with a "For Sale" sign in the front. Dad jumped out and pointed toward the back hatch. "Let me grab our stuff from the hotel."

Haddie slid out and opened the back. Crow, or his people, had packed her bags. Everyone's luggage, including Aaron's, lay in the back. She raised her eyebrows. "Didn't expect that."

Dad shrugged, grabbing his bag and Aaron's. "We already left enough evidence behind. I'm worried they're going to come looking for you."

She grabbed Kiana's duffel and followed him to the van. "You've got people watching me."

"That's all they'll do, watch. If the police or the FBI come for you, they won't get in the way." He tossed the bags inside. "You need to be careful. If anything seems out of the ordinary, get out."

Haddie laughed. "What in my life is ordinary?"

He shrugged. "You know what I mean." Pulling her close in a gentle hug, he said, "I love you."

"I love you too, Dad." Feeling a little less heavy, she walked Rock to the passenger side and let him in. Part of her held no hope for Josh; she'd seen the glow on the others after Lady Erica had disappeared. "Let's go, Boy. Time we got home."

Haddie played with her blackberry tart; she'd taken a bite but couldn't eat. She had enough makeup on that she felt like she wore Lady Erica's paint. The coffee shop, Roma's, smelled like coffee and cookies. *I should be hungry.* Her stomach hung on the edge of queasiness. Terry leaned his chair against the wall on the other side of the small table. Liz sat beside her.

"You okay? You don't look okay," Liz asked. "I don't mean —" She gestured over her face. "It was rough?"

Haddie nodded. Her head felt light, and her chest tingled. "I'll be okay."

Being back in her apartment had been relaxing. It would have been more so if Jisoo hadn't been screaming the entire time. She'd cried about Aaron and even losing Kiana to Dad's farm. The apartment felt empty.

"Glad you were able to come out for coffee," Haddie added.

Terry picked crumbs off his plate. "I've never been here before. Good scones."

Her heart raced in panic for a second. They hadn't

asked why she picked this place. She gestured toward her pastry, and he pulled it over to his side of the table with a finger.

"Josh?" asked Liz.

"I don't know." Haddie had called out of work that morning, and Toby had been sympathetic. Josh had called out as well. They had a new case. Boxes were stacking up in the back room. Haddie had missed two days. *I promised to be in tomorrow.* If she hadn't made plans, she would have gone to Josh's house today. Depending on how it went this afternoon, she might still make it there tonight. *I'm procrastinating.* Probably he wouldn't be any better, perhaps worse.

Haddie closed her eyes and felt Liz's hand on her shoulder.

Flakes dripped off Terry's lips as he asked, "Picked your schedule yet?"

School. The upcoming semester. "I haven't even looked." This would be her last year in law school. *I can't even think about that right now.* She did appreciate the change in topic. "You?"

"Locked in on Machine Language and Intermediate Algorithms. Thinking about Discrete Math. I need an Earth Science, not sure where to go with that one." Terry leaned in. "I'm looking for a late-night lab course. I want to work on a Faraday cage, but not at home, obviously."

Haddie glanced around the room. A couple sat quietly in the corner looking at their phones. A young woman sat across the room beside an archway with her Apple laptop and a "smash capitalism" sticker on the back. She could hear the two men sitting behind them, but they were laughing and joking, appearing not to pay any attention to them.

They would have to find another place and time to discuss everything that had gone on. This had truly been planned as a social gathering. *They want to know I'm okay.* They'd separately pushed for a meeting, and she planned on being here anyway.

Where are we going from here? She would miss the meetings at the hillside house. A lot of things would be different. Hopefully, the FBI wouldn't interfere with Terry. Detective Cooper still hounded her, looking for Dad. She needed some semblance of normalcy in her life. She needed game night and beers with Liz. Haddie bounced her leg and winced. It had been at least an hour. She checked her phone. *Twenty minutes.*

Liz looked at her and smirked. "When is he coming?"

"Who?" Terry asked.

"David," Haddie answered.

"Oh." Terry looked at Liz. "How'd you know?"

Liz tilted her head. "She's been going into bouts of panic. When?" she asked Haddie.

"Twenty minutes."

Terry nodded. "Do you want us to stay? For moral support."

"We're leaving in ten minutes." Liz wiped down the table with her napkin. "I feel better now that I got to see you. I'd still like to take some blood."

"Vampire," Terry said.

Haddie chuckled and took a deep breath, trying to push down her nerves. David had been open to meeting in the afternoon, and hadn't asked questions about the past few days. She'd thought he might not be available until after work, but it appeared his job was in Eugene this week and he could take time to meet. *What can I offer him in the long run?* She loved him. But her life would still be full of secrets, ones that could affect his life.

Most of all, he would grow old, and she would betray him by leaving him when it became obvious that she didn't age. *How can I do that?* How did Dad do that? He was right that she couldn't spend her life avoiding love, but how could she accept the inevitable? *Could she let him in, as she had with Liz and Terry?*

"Bye, Haddie." Liz stood up. She opened her arms and Haddie rose for a hug.

Terry offered a fist bump. "Later, Buckaroo."

Alone, Haddie watched the door. Then she went and got another tea. Sitting back down, she checked her phone. *Three minutes.* The woman with the Apple laptop swore at her screen, "Bastard." The couple had left. The men behind Haddie had left.

Outside, David walked past the window wearing a tight, light-green polo shirt. He looked in the window, but not as far back as she sat. Her heart raced. *I don't need to be nervous.* She waited, hearing the front door chime. The wall separating the front entrance and counter from the sitting area blocked her view, but she imagined his footsteps on the tile. The arched opening had two windowed sections on each side, so they spotted each other through the window first.

His face, tight along the jaw, softened; his cheeks rose, causing the lines around his eyes to crease, and then his lips pursed into a happy, almost shy smile. They locked eyes and the wood of the arch faded. The counter attendant called out a greeting, but David ignored them, striding through the arch toward Haddie.

In his right hand, he carried a small white lily. A florist's tube clung to the end of the stem. He'd bought her flowers before, but a bouquet would have seemed overbearing in front of these strangers. *A single flower is sweet.* Her breath caught. *I don't deserve this.*

Haddie rose, with her stomach queasy and knees that threatened to betray her.

David didn't hand her the flower; he placed it on the table and took her in his arms. "I've missed you." He pulled tightly against her and exhaled with a peaceful sigh in her ear. She could feel his heart pounding against her chest.

"I'm sorry," she breathed.

"No. I demanded." His lips brushed against her shoulder, on the slim bare section before her powdered neck. "I don't need to know all your secrets. I just need to know that you want me. That will be enough. I promise."

"I love you." She fought the tears. How could she do this to him? *I can't* not *love him.*

"I love you," he said. His hands rose up her back, loosening their almost desperate grip to become a light trace along her shoulder blades. David pulled back to see her, and his fingers drifted through her hair until they held her face. Tenderly, they pulled her lips to his. He kissed her as if they were alone.

The cafe and the world disappeared. Her fears and protests dissolved. *I can't fight this.* If he could accept her secrets, then she would give him everything else she could.

When they finally separated, she looked into the brown depths of his eyes. They could have years before she would have to hide her inability to age. Dad had done it.

He looked at her gloved hand on his shoulder. "The rash?"

"Yes," she lied.

HADDIE PULLED up to the trailer behind Josh's black Jeep. She placed her RAV4 into park, turned it off, and sat in the silence for a moment. Dry gardens fought weeds around an off-white trailer with brown trim, but they looked as if at one time they'd been cared for. A blue birdbath had a dull ring in the bottom where water had once been kept. The wood porch had clear plastic sheeting attached to the overhang to keep the rain out. Empty pots were lined behind the plastic.

Haddie found Josh's glow sitting behind the Jeep in the carport ahead of her. A shed attached to the back had a door open. His haze seemed to be positioned there. *What is he doing?*

Haddie stepped out. Even early in the morning it felt stifling hot. The weather promised rain, but not until later in the afternoon.

Andrea had been happy to let Haddie leave to check on Josh. He called in dutifully each day, but hadn't shown up since the weekend. *Since we killed Lady Erica.*

Haddie walked along the far side of the driveway,

avoiding the tight confines between the Jeep and the porch. Josh sat in an old lawn chair with a book in his lap. He looked up, dully surprised to see her.

"Hi, Josh." Haddie stepped into the shade of the carport, a pace or two in front of him. Inside the shed, books lined shelves, two deep in most places.

"Hi." He responded without any emotion. *Does he even know who I am?* "It's Haddie."

"Yes," he said.

He didn't look dirty or unkempt. His wild blond hair even looked combed. She hadn't been sure what to expect. *Depraved, that was what I expected.* She remembered the lady sitting in the parking lot. Had all of Lady Erica's people lost any sense of drive? At least he read, that implied some level of self-care.

"What are you reading?"

"*Wheel of Time* by Robert Jordan." He held the book up briefly, then placed it back on his lap.

"We need you at work."

He looked to the book. "I have nothing left to do."

"What do you mean?"

"I did everything I was supposed to. What do I do now?" He touched the pages of the book, as if feeling for an answer there.

Did he mean he fulfilled Lady Erica's instructions? Did he hang in limbo, waiting for the next assignment? It wouldn't come, at least not from her. Could others control him?

"Are you waiting for her?"

Jerking his head up, he nodded, almost pleading, as if Haddie might have news on her absence.

"Can you go back to work, while you wait?" Josh

deserved some sense of normalcy. "Can someone else give you instructions?"

He leaned back, frowning. "Tyrone."

Was that Lady Erica's assistant? He wouldn't be bringing any messages either.

In this condition, Josh would end up homeless, living or dying on the streets. Was this the fate of all the innocents who had been coerced? She couldn't save them all. Killing Lady Erica had doomed them.

Haddie knelt down, wincing. "Josh, I saw Lady Erica this weekend."

His eyes widened and he sat straighter.

She swallowed. "She wants you to go back to your life. Wait for her next command. Until then, you need to do everything you always did. No one can know."

It took a moment, but he took in a deep breath and stood.

Haddie scrambled back. She blushed at her reaction. He didn't pose a threat, coerced or not.

Josh stepped inside the shed and slid the book onto one of the shelves deliberately. Stepping back outside, he shut the shed door and locked it. It appeared her statement had worked. Without a word he folded up the chair, leaned it against the shed, and strode for the porch of his trailer. He seemed to be taking her directions. What did he need inside? Keys? Wallet?

She swallowed. Did Josh feel his mother's death? At least, her absence?

Haddie watched as he stepped inside the empty trailer. His yellow haze, visible through the wall, headed toward the back. *Still coerced. He's not free, but he might live.* Her throat felt thick. She'd not saved Josh, not completely.

When he pulled out in his Jeep, Haddie followed him

back to the office. They met in the parking lot without a word between them.

Haddie felt as lost and empty as Josh looked. *I don't know what I can do, but I haven't given up.* The chime to the front door of the office rang as she stepped inside.

If you haven't read the Origin story, *Shattered Blood*, then download a free ebook or purchase the paperback or audible on Amazon.

AngelSong Series

Penumbra - Book One

Red Tempest - Book Two

Coerced - Book Three

Demons' Lair - Book Four

Infrared - Book Five. (End of the AngelSong Series)

Website KevinArthurDavis.com

Facebook @KevinArthurDavis

Please join my mailing list if you'd like to be kept up to date on this series and the upcoming Khimmer Chronicles series.

ACKNOWLEDGMENTS

My wife April continues to support me in my writing career. That includes long hours listening to audible reviews and unending plans, ideas, and concerns that I might imagine.

Robyn Huss, my editor, has an amazing (magical?) ability to transform my words into a better version of my ideas. Because she doesn't have time to get to all my work, I've tried a dozen editors and she outshines them.

I will dearly miss a beloved and irreplaceable mentor, David Farland; our loss is felt around the world. Please pick up one of his books and enjoy the magic he endowed upon the world. Writers, study his lessons at Apex Writers.

Jody Lynn Nye's workshop does wonders for many aspiring writers.

My writing groups from JordanCon, DragonCon, and Apex are fundamental in making sure I keep on track.

Thank you.

www.ingramcontent.com/pod-product-compliance
Lightning Source LLC
Chambersburg PA
CBHW061610190726
48288CB00007B/2262